About the Author

Jon-Jon was born Jon Stephen Jones in the south midlands, UK in 1976 and now lives in central London. He has always had a love of reading and particularly enjoys the adventure classics as well as children's.

As well as Tiger! Tiger! Tiger! Jon-Jon has also written a collection of short stories called Victorian Adventure Stories, a children's book series entitled Aaron the Alien, a Children's novel called The Jellyset Kid as well as poetry and a blog.

For more information on Jon-Jon please visit:

www.Jon-Jon.co.uk

For his Aaron the Alien series visit

www.AarontheAlien.com

For all those who are dedicated to saving the tiger; especially the people that live in real fear of the mighty and beautiful *Panthera Tigris* yet do not harbour any animosity against it.

Also for my parents who never stop believing in me.

TIGER!

TIGER!

TIGER!

By Jon-Jon
(J S Jones)

Copyright Notice

This book is copyright material and must not be copied, reproduced, transferred, distributed, leased, licensed or publicly performed or used in any way except as specifically permitted in writing by the author, as allowed under terms and conditions under which it was purchased or as strictly permitted by applicable copyright law. Any unauthorised distribution or use of this text may be a direct infringement of the author's rights and those responsible maybe liable in law accordingly.

The moral right of Jon Stephen Jones – Jon-Jon to be identified as the author of this work has been asserted in accordance with the Copyright, Designs & Patents Act 1988

Copyright © 2016 Jon Stephen Jones – Jon-Jon
All Rights Reserved

This book is a work of fiction. Names, characters, places and incidents are either a product of the authors imagination or used fictitiously. Any resemblance to actual people living or dead, events or locales is entirely coincidental.
Ebooks are not transferable.

Library of Congress Control Number

The Thrill of the Chase
TX0008257588
The Fallen & the Missing/The Great Tiger King
TXu002013779

Cover by
www.damonza.com

CONTENTS

Volume I

The Thrill of the Chase 1

Volume II

The Fallen and the Missing 37

Volume III

The Great Tiger King 102

Tiger! Tiger! Tiger!

Volume I

The Thrill of the Chase

The fan whirred noisily in the vacuous ceiling space. Eggshell painted walls adorned the large room that was laced with wicker furniture and tables that sported square glass hats. Exotic trees and plants littered this aerated bar area of the old colonial hotel.

A mixologist dressed in a white tuxedo stood firmly, awaiting orders. There were not many people in the bar at this time of morning, an old English colonel sat there having morning tea with his longstanding wife.

Tea in this hotel was no ordinary business; brewed at a perfect temperature and for a precise amount of time, sterling silver tea pots and the finest bone china cups. It was made at your tableside from fresh leaves, strained through a filter and poured by a qualified server who had tea making mastered to an exact science.

The old Colonel and his wife sat there talking genially in their thin attire, across the room there was a solitary man sitting at a table by himself, but he was not drinking tea, he was drinking a fifteen year old whisky.

The man had on a traditional khaki uniform, he was of aristocratic appearance. His khaki pith helmet lay on one of the empty chairs. He was a tall, thin man, with a particularly prognathous nose. His head easily showed the facial structure of his jaw and skull, his eyeballs were sunken in their sockets; the skin of his face pulled so tight that it seemed every feature was accentuated. Dark greyish hair receded creating a large visible forehead.

He was in his late forties, lithe and energetic. He sat in the chair perfectly composed, enjoying his whisky with ice that had been shipped all the way from the arctic. Even his posture seemed to read opulence. A bottle of the illustrious firewater was on the table and an ice bucket sat next to him like an obedient dog.

A kerfuffle roused his attention away from the relaxed state he was in. A party of three men entered the bar through the historic tall single pane glass doors that were nearly all glass except for the wooden panels that covered the bottom fifth. They talked noisily, one of the men surveyed the room with confidence and upon seeing the solitary drinker, the man waved his finger and proceeded straight towards him.

'Charles, how the devil are you?' Charles put down his whisky glass and stood to greet the party.

'Gerald, always a pleasure.' he said extending his hand. Gerald shook his hand, he was of a similar height to Charles but stockier, his face was not so gaunt, shocks of black hair peeked out from underneath a Panama style hat.

A man with a florid face and ginger hair stepped forward, he was athletic and muscular. 'George,' said Charles leaning forward and shaking his hand.

'Hello Robert, good to see you again,' replied Charles to the fourth man, who was shorter and of medium build with brown parted hair. He sported a thin moustache.

'I see you are celebrating Charles.' said Gerald.

'Absolutely.' said Charles clicking his fingers at the man behind the bar. 'Three glasses please and be quick about it.' The Barman did a shallow bow and motioned to someone else out of view.

'Come, come, sit down gentlemen.' Charles beckoned, waving his hand towards the empty seats; the three men sat down. 'Please join me, I insist.'

'Is that …' Robert said leaning over and picking up the bottle '… that's an old bottle of *Black & White*, good grief man.'

'That is correct, I brought several cases years back, put them in storage and forgot to drink them, if it's good enough for the king.'

'King George drinks it?' asked Robert

'His father Edward certainly did.' replied George

'I insist that you help yourselves it is a glorious day and I am what you might say 'on top of the world.'' said Charles.

'And your game!' Gerald said.

Charles found this most amusing and leaning forward slapped Gerald on the shoulder. 'Where is this damn waiter?' Charles snapped, looking annoyed as he stared towards the bar.

'He does like to celebrate in style, which is why we insist on hearing any good news immediately,' said George. This comment created a small cacophony of laughter between Gerald and George.

'So what is it that we are celebrating?' asked Robert.

'Ah finally.' said Charles as the waiter appeared also wearing a white tux with a Turban adorning his head. 'Really! You do not keep a man waiting when he has something to celebrate.' Charles' face began to redden slightly.

'Apologies sir.' said the waiter, bowing slightly.

'Well, serve my good friends and we shall call the matter settled.'

The waiter put three fingers of the extravagant scotch into the crystal tumblers, using a pair of tongs he dropped in a couple of large rocks of ice. After placing the drinks on ivory coasters, he bowed again and departed in silence.

'Well gentlemen, the curiosity is most confounding, will you not speak?'

'Ah, yes of course I will, apologies Robert, I assumed you knew, as Gerald and George did.'

'You must forgive me if I seem obtuse for not enquiring further, prior to our arrival, but the excitement of our previous conversation commanded my mind somewhat. Albeit I was indeed told that you would be in a celebratory mood. Had a windfall or something old chap?'

'Not quite, you enjoy hunting and game Robert? I assume you do since the company you keep.'

'Yes I do and I am aware that you are a keen hunter yourself.' said Robert raising his foot up on to his knee.

'Indeed I am.' returned Charles topping up his glass with some ice and two fingers of Whisky.'

'He's a fanatic.' chimed in George returning his drink to the table.

'Well I am keen, yes.'

'*Keen*, come, come Charles, you speak as if we do not know our quarry. I am convinced there are more animals hanging from your walls than there are roaming the jungle.' said Gerald with a rather high spiritedness.

George and Robert laughed, while Charles smiled gaily.

'Alas the guilty has been found, but any man of character should enjoy a good hunt.' retorted Charles.

'Here, here,' said Robert holding up his glass before having a sip.

'So tell me Robert, what do you think the ultimate catch would be in these parts.'

'An elephant?' Robert replied.

'*An Elephant*.' They are big and clumsy, where is the skill in that? I assure you, it is not an elephant that has eluded me all these years.' said Charles throwing his arms in the air.

Robert sat there for a minute and stroked his thin moustache, 'a tiger!'

'Precisely Robert, and what a magnificent beast it is. I have been trying to get one for the past ten years and I have finally succeeded, he will be a rug on my floor before the week is out, but I shall make sure he has pride of place, so all the visitors may relish in my triumph.'

'Congratulations, my dear fellow how happy you must be.'

'Happy, I could not contain myself old man, I tell you, I was straight on the phone to George and Gerald …'

'Yelping like a school boy he was.' said George, enjoying the story.

'I will excuse myself of vigorous expostulations on this occasion gentleman, it is every hunters dream to tackle the fiercest beasts, a *tiger* is as cunning as it is fierce.'

'So come on Charles give us the details, as in your excitement last night you said only that you had finally slew 'the great cat.''

'Outstanding whisky, great crowd, accompanied by an adventure of the grandest proportions – why ever not old chap.' said Robert making himself comfortable.

'But, before I start, I am afraid I must insist that you indulge in the pleasure set before us.' said Charles.

'Really, I must protest Charles, it is still well in the morning, to let any inebriation take hold would be most irregular.' remonstrated Gerald.

'I agree with Gerald, Charles, but we will gladly listen to your most singular story.' said George placing his half empty drink upon the table as if his body language were betraying his true feelings on the matter.

'Nonsense Gentlemen, another two fingers each, that is all I ask. You might need it, as I will be asking of your services this very day, we will not be sitting round like drunkards and dullards if I have anything to do with it.'

The three men looked at each other with curious eyes.

Charles had already started putting extra ice in all their glasses, the three men sat there kind of dumbfounded at the insistence of their friend; their bemusement continued as the fine amber transparent fire water doused the freshly laid frost ridden rocks.

'We shall join you in this drink Charles for we count ourselves in good company but as fine as your intentions are any more drinks this morning would be an aberration.' said Gerald in a resolute tone.

'I can assure you gentleman that I am the arguments biggest advocate, I merely wish to enjoy this special occasion and prepare myself for the adventure ahead. Anymore and I would spoil my own enjoyment, perhaps even endanger the success of my next enterprise.

However if you are all ready then I will begin my symposium. I set off early yesterday morning, although the elephant is a great tradition and albeit it can get to a lot more places, I ended up opting for the speed of a mechanical vehicle. Simply because if you know roughly where the tiger was last sighted and you get there rapidly you vastly increase your chances.

I know what you must think gentleman that once out of the vehicle it is anyone's game; but as you shall see I am not one who fears easily, not when I have so comprehensively mastered the rifle that I hold.

Anyway there had been reports of some fresh tiger tracks about twenty miles to the east, and as George and Gerald will tell you Robert, I demand that I am informed immediately if any such evidence becomes apparent. I took my trusty manservant and a guide who I have regularly employed for some years and we set off. It was a clear morning yesterday and not ten minutes into the journey I saw vultures circling overhead, this I took for a good sign.

The guide as ever had been prolific in his investigations and he quickly determined the exact spot where the tiger must have been last. Fortunately for us the dirt track that he crossed, was only a couple of kilometres in from the main road so the majority of the journey was made with considerable alacrity.

We bumped along the dirt track, when the guide ordered my manservant to halt. The guide jumped out of the vehicle and started to inspect the track, it was not long before he came across some fresh paw prints and deduced - by whatever powers these remarkable men work by – that it was probably a couple of hours ago.

I remember sighing deeply, I was hoping he would say half an hour maybe even an hour, this really extended the realistic range that I would to try to cover to find my quarry. The guide however, was far from satisfied and started walking up the track. We let him continue walking and watched as he slowly plodded off, just as he was starting to reach the horizon, he gesticulated at us excitedly. I ordered that we drive up to him.

I leapt out of the *Rolls* to see what had the man so excitable.

'Five minutes.' he shouted.

'Five minutes.' he shouted again.

'Five minutes?' I asked and then joy leapt across my face at the realisation of what he was showing me, there were fresh tiger tracks and they were only made five minutes ago, I was overjoyed, ran straight to the car and got my hunting rifle.

'The tiger must have come across just before we appeared.' The guide informed me, it was then that he got up and walked slowly to the edge of the tree line, he stood still for a moment and then started sniffing, walking from tree to tree, bending down at each one.

'Looking for scratch marks?' enquired Robert, interrupting Charles's monologue.

'No.' said Charles. Trying to remember where he was in his story. Robert noted Charles' slight annoyance, at his ill-timed heckle.

'He was sniffing for scent?'

'Exactly George, as I was saying he continued along the tree line when he suddenly threw his head up in disgust, he beckoned me over to the tree. Of course being an enthusiast when it comes to hunting I knew why he was calling me over, so without instruction I leant over to inhale what I could. The smell was so repugnant that I nearly wretched. I thought I had had many close encounters with these ferocious felines, but the strength of the odour made me wonder whether I had been disillusioned all along.'

'Whatever you do mean dear fellow?' asked Gerald leaning forward to obtain his drink.

'What I mean gentleman, is in all my years of what I deem to be 'The Great Hunt' I had always smelled the Tiger's markings and I had presumed I was close on their trail, but the very strength of this particular marking made me wonder whether I ever had been that close at all.

It was at this point that the guide grabbed my arm, to gain my full attention, I wondered his intention for a minute and then he looked at me urgently.

'Sir make sure your rifle is ready and you are prepared, these markings were made only minutes ago for all we know the beast could be watching us right now.'

I cocked my rifle and adjusted it so I could carry it in a ready to fire position. I then signalled the manservant to stay with the car and headed into the dense jungle, taking the lead I quietly crept forward, scanning the periphery as I did.

The guide followed me in, which I allowed as he might be of some help, within a minute or two, I was proved right when he tapped me on the shoulder and silently gesticulated up in the trees, I immediately understood his alarm as tigers are capable climbers and they are often found hiding in trees.

Proceeding with caution and confident that with two keen observers we should be able to find the elusive predator, I marched slowly through foliage aware that the beast could have gone only a few steps in any direction and disappeared from view. I have no idea what it was, perhaps some form of hunter's instinct but I veered to the left. I remember the foliage suddenly became rather thick and I grew concerned that we were creating the sounds of a tumultuous marching band.

I stepped slowly over a fallen log and pushed away some giant leaves and right in front of my eyes were *two* tigers laying side by side …'

'*Two*!' exclaimed George.

'Yes, two my good friend and neither were shy of size either. They were a little way off, as I had happened upon a small clearing and were camped straight across from me on the other side. I do not mind confessing to you that I was giddy with exhilaration and happiness, I wanted to relish the moment and after all these years savour the opportunity. I taunted myself that perhaps I could get closer to add a more personal and victorious touch, but my senses quickly returned when I realised that I had my dream right in front of my eyes and I could not risk losing it.

I took aim; I could not tell which was the larger as they were both big, even for Tigers. Wasting no more time I fired, hitting one in the chest as it lay down, it tried to get up and run away but it couldn't, it just collapsed, I think it died right then and there. The other one was gone before I could even get off another shot. But that did not phase me gentlemen. I fancy I shall never admit this again but I could even testify that a skip entered my gait as I traversed the long grass to my reward.

At last Gentleman, I had hunted, stalked and killed my most prized quarry. I could live the rest of my life at ease knowing that I had achieved one of my most excitable and rewarding goals.

I did a quick look for the other cat but knew there was no point as it would have cleared the area with considerable immediacy.

'What a splendid story.' said Robert stroking his moustache with his index finger and thumb.

'Here, here.' said George, nodding his glass towards Charles.

'Your most enjoyable hunting story yet Charles, you are to be congratulated upon what you have achieved.' said Gerald.

'Your words are most kind gentleman, but perhaps we should consider more, what I'm about to achieve.'

'About to achieve? Whatever do you mean old man?' Gerald said, scratching his shin with his other foot.

'Well you will recall earlier that - I need … or rather - I would like - to call upon your services, on this very day, indeed in this very hour. The truth is that last night after the expensive Champagne and cigars I enjoyed with my guide and manservant - as I did not want to hinder yourselves at such a late hour you understand - I climbed into my bed and in my quasi relaxed state an intruder crept into my mind and began to haunt me, it robbed me of my elation and I was vexed to realise so. It was the other tiger of course.'

'Come, come Charles' said Robert leaning forward and putting his drink down on the table. 'This really will not do, you have just told the most extraordinary tale I have heard and you end it with a revelation like that. How many people have actually successfully set out to hunt a tiger and done so – nary there be such a man in this country I can tell you.'

'Gentlemen, gentlemen, you waste your time on a worthless argument. I have been holding back a shameful secret from you, the tiger that I killed yesterday was the female and although it was still a joyous occasion it was not the pinnacle of a hunter's career that I had hoped for. Why at that very second last night in bed I decided that I would find and kill this alpha male like any hunter would and give him pride of place along with his friend. Look at it this way; they will not be alone will they?' Charles grinned and gave a little chuckle at his remark.

'Do not let the male detract from your success the tigress is still a magnificent beast.' said Gerald removing his hat and placing it in his lap in an almost pleading gesture.

'My decision is already made, I must say I am surprised by your attitude Gerald, to the hunter the sex is everything you always want it to be the alpha male, otherwise it could look like you went for the lesser competition.' said Charles, awkwardly fidgeting in his seat.

'Normally I would completely agree,' said George, 'but there is *no* shame when it comes to tigers, especially ones the size of which you encountered. Myself and Gerald have both been to see your prize possession before we called on Robert to join our tryst.'

'I have to say Charles, you will not be able not tell the difference when it is decorating your floor anyway, Why hunt another one? You have already achieved glory as you quite rightly pointed out at the beginning of your anecdote.'

'Why hunt another Robert? Why hunt another? When a man goes to war does he just seek one medal, of course not, he continues, well this is the same thing. When that tiger ran off he challenged me and mark my words sir, I will sell his bones and keep his skin.' said Charles, staring incredulously at Robert whilst leaning forward as if the question had greatly affronted him.

'Control your fiery iniquities Charles, it will not do.' said George.

'Yes ... well ... excuse me ... but never question a hunter on why he does what he does, it is his instinct and there is nothing more than that in the man.'

'Well said.' said Gerald clapping his hands, 'although I fear you put even the most ardent hunter to shame.'

'Well, do you accept my invitation gentlemen?'

'By Jove, you want us to join you on the hunt?' said Robert.

'Of course I do, will you not all join me?' Charles looked and smiled at Robert. Robert nodded at him having realised Charles was as hot and interchangeable as the liquor they had been drinking.

'You know me old sport, where there is adventure there is always George Harris.'

'You need not ask me Charles you should know that by now.' said Gerald.

'And I will certainly come.' said Robert sitting up in his seat.

'Excellent, then the matter is sorted gentlemen, we shall set out shortly, please finish your drinks first though, as this should give us enough of the spirit of adventure to be getting on with.'

'How will you know that it is the right tiger?' said Robert really savouring the whisky from his glass.

'Outstanding Master Robert, we will make a hunter out of you yet. There was a detail I omitted from my earlier report. One of the tigers had a long gash down the front of his leg, nothing to impede it, superficial, but easily visible in its current state due to the flesh still being exposed. It must have been done recently and fortunately for me it was the one who got away who bore it.'

'Excellent spot Charles, that is a useful bit of knowledge.'

'Yes I thought so as well. I was so distracted by my prize kill that before the dream last night I did not even think of going back out for the male tiger. I must say I am glad that he paid me a visit last night, lest he get away. There is one condition to my request.'

'Oh what is that?' said George scratching his ginger hair.

'That I be the man who kills the beast of course.'

'Why, should a man steal your honour in such a fashion I would shoot him myself.'

'Why thank you Robert, most kind.'

'We will not even hunt, just observe. Again I am surprised you should even ask such a question.' said George.

'I confess to you all that this great *panthera tigris* has me in a tither but before the day is out he will be mine.' Charles stood up alarmingly quick. Robert tensed for a second for he was not used to his quick actions, Charles held up his glass with a straight arm in the air going into the middle of the table and his companions.

They all stood up and held their glasses in the air as if they were going to create some four ring symbolic logo.

'*To the tiger.*' said George.

'*To the hunt.*' said Gerald.

'*To the kill.*' said Robert.

'*To the thrill of the chase.*' said Charles and as soon as he did their glasses all clinked and the four men downed the last of their drinks.

The men were all appropriately attired with comfortable hard wearing trousers and shirts adorned with pockets. They wore tough jungle boots on their feet.

'I rather suspect you had some pre-eminent inclinations.' said Charles as the party walked through the double doors straight into a wall of heat.

'Charles, we know your proclivities too well, myself and George do anyway and I'm sure Robert is a quick study.'

The party were surprised to find the vehicle waiting, with Charles' guide and manservant already aboard. It was a customized, dark green *Rolls Royce Silver Ghost*. The back end of the car had been extended out to create an extra row of seats and the wheels were slightly larger. Boxes and packs were strapped to the over-hanging shelf that was bolted to the rear end of the vehicle, the tyres looked more suited to a tractor this made the carriage set higher above the ground than usual.

Hunting could be a very dangerous prospect; in a land where even plants and insects could kill, preparation was vital.

The manservant was in the driving seat. They were both Indian men, the driver was a tall bearded man wearing a dark red turban whilst the guide was a clear skinned man in his thirties, his hair was shone jet black and was brushed to the side with surprising precision.

'I think it would be suggestible for me to get some of my small arms to bring with us strictly as a safety precaution.' said George.

'No need gentlemen.' I have ensured that the car is fully stocked we have plenty of munitions including rifles, pistols and the back is stocked with all manner of supplies including food and drink.' said Charles as he nodded to the guide who immediately disembarked and presented four gun belts out of a canvas bag. The four men took them with alacrity, it was then they were handed a six shot revolver each with a box of bullets.

'Careful, the guns are already loaded.'

'Excellent.' said Gerald snapping his barrel shut.

To their surprise the guide then pulled out four hunting knives and handed them over, it was only then they realised that there was a place, to holster the blade on the other side.

'Just had these hunting belts shipped over the other day, I thought it would be a good time to give them a trial.' said Charles, slotting the blade in its scab. He climbed aboard and placed a small box of bullets in a perfectly fitting pouch on the belt which the others duly noted and copied his actions. He sat behind the guide who had returned to the front passenger seat.'

George climbed in and sat next to him and then Gerald climbed in behind Charles with Robert sitting behind George.

Charles tapped his manservant on the shoulder and they set off down the road, the effects of the whisky were evident, for the men were in high spirits and eagerly trying to outdo each other with stories of hunting and adventure.

The heat was stifling but the breeze of the journey soon cooled them down. The guide and the manservant joined the conversation primarily at a prompting from Charles.

'So how did you get into hunting Charles?' asked Robert leaning forward, shouting from the back seat.

'It goes back to your childhood doesn't it, Charles.' said Gerald with a smile on his face.

'Confound you Gerald, shouting a man's business about like that, have you no sensibility man.' Charles said, his face florid.

Gerald chuckled at his deliberate remark, a smile crossed George's face too.

'Oh damn you both I will have to tell him now, you know I do not like discussing such things.' said Charles.

'Apologies Sir Charles, I meant not to cause any discontent between you.' Robert replied leaning forward and putting his hand on Charles's shoulder.

'Don't be so foolish Robert you were not to know.' Charles said as he threw a suspicious glance toward Gerald and George.

'No good looking at us old sport.' said George with a semi-serious look on his face.

'I grew up on a country estate deep in rural England. My father, a stern Victorian man was an ardent hunter in his own right. Such was his passion that he forced it on to me and my brother …'

'And you took to it right away?' interrupted Robert.

'Really man, what is wrong with you, do you want to hear this story or not?'

'… uh … yes of course I do.' replied Robert meekly.

'As I was saying hunting was forced upon us as a requirement, not just for food, which was sometimes provided for by our gains, but also for status, to be a gentleman.

You are quite mistaken by your assumption Robert as it was my brother Henry who was quick on the uptake, I had no such desire believe it not. Of course this was not to be tolerated and every time my father and brother went shooting I was to accompany them.'

'I think a lot of us had fathers like that in one way or another.' said George.

'Yes quite.' added Gerald.

'My brother and I shared the usual sibling rivalry but the balance of favour was always tipped toward him and even when I did upend my brother through some feat of victory it was inevitably hunting that mattered most with my father.

I remember once gloating that I had a better mark than my brother for a school report, as he had done to me on numerous occasions, just as I felt that at last I had gained the upper hand, my father remarked 'Well done, but let's not forget your brother is going to become a damn fine hunter.'

This grieved my young mind considerably as my brother usually bested me at most things and he never held back in gloating and taunting. Hunting was always the card up his sleeve that swayed my father's approval. It goes without saying that if by any chance my father forgot to bring it up, my sibling wouldn't.

Ironically the one subject I excelled in was nature, it wasn't the countryside that had no interest for me it was just the hunt. Nature and art were always on my mind, I learned to track animals in order to watch or draw them. My mother had noticed this but my father and brother were too pre-occupied to register my budding talent.

The thought of hunting to impress my father began to thrash around in my head like an eagle trapped in a cage. It was a winter's morning when things finally changed, we had been hunting and Reginald had shot three rabbits to my none. I however was without interest, the plummeting temperature had me too distracted, but he gloated and gloated and rather than remonstrating with him my father picked him up and held him aloft like a trophy, in that very minute something in me snapped gentlemen and I vowed to become the best hunter a man could become.

The very next time we went out, the onset of spring was just beginning. I was determined, full of concentration, all the things I had learned while trying to watch and draw wildlife in my younger years came to together in some sort of epiphany. As we embarked on the hunt, I watched and saw, walked and found, shot and hit.

I swear I shot almost everything on an Englishman's hunting menu that day.'

'What on earth did your father say?' asked Gerald.

'I remember him looking at me after comparing our quarries, he bursting out laughing telling me that he always knew there was something special in me and then he held *me* up high. There was no shortage of gloating in *me* that day I can tell you.'

Everyone in the *Rolls Royce* laughed including the guide and driver in the front of the vehicle.

'Please continue I am rather enjoying the story.' said the driver.

'I must confess I am also embroiled in your childhood tale Charles.' said Robert.

'After that my progress was rapid, it seems I could just hunt, my skills rapidly became that of my Fathers and soon surpassed them. I studied it every moment I had you understand but it was built on an early and solid foundation, I still believe to this day that that has always given me the edge.

The next thing you know my father was showing me off at country fairs and tournaments, I was in the newspaper and as my trophy cabinet filled I gloated all the more.' Charles sighed deeply. 'It wasn't until adulthood that I finally relented my torturous and vengeful diatribes upon my sibling.'

Charles had stopped talking but there was silence in the vehicle, everyone it seemed was on tenterhooks. With a stoical expression Charles continued.

'Many years after that my brother and I discussed it, to my astonishment he apologised to *me*, stating that he did not realise how cruel he had been until it was visited upon himself, albeit it grated him after a while that I would not cease, he said he was - in the end, nevertheless grateful.'

'So you ended up the favourite son then?'

'Not quite, my brother stayed close to my father as hunting ever increasingly took me to faraway lands. It was my brother who stood beside him in his frail age. We had seemingly grown apart but my father's death brought us together again. It was only after we had put that great man in the ground that my brother told me father had repented to him, my father went on to explain that despite his foolish bragging he never thought one better than the other, he was just eager for us to succeed.'

Silence hung in the vehicle, despite the refreshing breeze and the bumpiness of the road the atmosphere was somehow still.

'It's funny, sometimes the thing that is meant to help is what hurts us the most.' said George leaning forward speaking quietly.

'Well you're certainly an outstanding *Shikari* now old chap.' said Gerald with a smile.

'Well that's enough of this nonsense, driver are we there yet? What is taking so bloody long.'

Their voices were often raised as the noise of the motor car competed against them, traffic was not really issue in this part of the world, most roads were dirt tracks and only distinguished by varying grades of bumps and drivability.

The *Silver Ghost* finally turned off the dirt road and onto the even bumpier track where Charles had encountered the tigers the previous day.

'Stop where we did yesterday.' said Charles.

'Yes Sir,' said the driver without taking his eye off the road.

The guide suddenly shouted stop.

'What is it?'

'Look at the trees.'

'Good God, he's right, the scratch marks, look at the size of them.'

'Scratch marks?' enquired Robert.

'Yes, they were made a by a tiger and a huge one as well by the look of it.' added George.

'Come on. Time to learn gentlemen.' said Charles informing the driver to stay with the car at all times as there were a lot of supplies on there that needed guarding.

'Yes sir, you can depend on me.' The driver replied.

They approached the trees, Robert gasped as he saw the size of the claws that had easily slashed open the tree.

'Are you sure we're not hunting a dinosaur?' asked Robert stepping back from the tree slightly.

'Not a dinosaur but it sure is a bloody big cat.' said Charles laughing loudly. The others joined in with the exception of the guide who just smiled at the camaraderie.

'I would say it's a very large male, it passed not that long ago may be an hour or so, maybe less, and it was headed along the roadside in the direction we are headed.'

They walked along the grass following the giant claw marks straddled across the largest of trees, the driver started the engine and followed along the road at a slow pace.

Charles suddenly burst into an urgent stride.

'Here gentlemen, here is the tree where the scent was, that is right isn't it?'

'Yes, Sir that is the tree.' The guide said pulling out a canteen of water and drinking from it.

'What do you think, shall we get straight into the hunt?'

'That would not be a very good idea, we are in the heat of the day and the tiger will be sleeping.' The guide said.

'He is right, you know Charles.'

'He had ought to be, that is what he is paid for. But while the tiger is resting he will not be getting further away from us.' replied Charles.

'That is true, as long as we head in the right direction.' said Robert.

'What do you think Gerald?'

Gerald took off his straw panama style hat and wiped his forehead, his black hair shone in the bright sun, the air was filled with the sounds of the jungle and heat lines danced on the horizon. 'I think we should check the area where the tigers were yesterday, this should enable us to think about where and when to start tracking.'

'Yes perhaps you are right but I cannot bear the thought of not hunting down that cat.'

'Patience Charles, I tell you man, you are already starting to become obsessed and it cannot lead to anything good.' said George.

'*Pah*, I just want what should be mine.' said Charles flicking his hand away. 'Come, let me show you where I slew its friend yesterday.'

'Would you like me to arrange some refreshment for when you get back Sir.' said the driver silently appearing.

'I say you have quite the skill of sneaking up.' said George.

'One should always move with grace sir.' The driver replied stoically.

'Yes why not, we shall go and investigate and then return for some luncheon but til then we hunt with vigour.' Charles said.

'Very good sir.' said the driver offering a shallow bow and returning to the vehicle.

Gerald looked round at George and Robert and then back to Charles. 'Sounds like a good plan to us old man.'

'Excellent, follow me.' Charles said stepping confidently into the jungle, they pushed their way through the foliage until they reached the place at the edge of the clearing.

'This is where I was standing and you see across there near that fallen tree, that was where the tigers were; they must have thought they were safe.' said Charles chuckling to himself.

'Look you can see the blood from where we dragged the carcass back through.' said the guide pointing to some flattened grass that was stained with blood.

'It must have been a good shot from here to fell it in one Charles.' said Robert putting his hand over his eyes to see across the small plain.

'I would have said so as well, thank you Robert.' said Charles pulling out a handkerchief and mopping his brow.'

'Shall we go and see the exact spot.' said Gerald.

'Why of course we will old boy. Do follow.' Charles said looking round and noticing that the guide was distracted by the shrubbery.

'Are you coming?' Charles asked. The guide looked straight up at him. 'Yes ... let us proceed.'

The party walked through the tall grass to the spot where the tigers had been laying, there was still blood on the floor and you could see where the corpse had been dragged out the day previous.

Led by Charles, they walked straight into the area.

'Really, please gentlemen, you employ me to do a job.' said the guide throwing his hands in the air.

'Quite right, apologies my good man.' said Charles beckoning everyone back out of the spot.

'I am surprised that tigers are brave enough to venture on the paths and roads.' said Robert, still looking at the grisly scene.

'Why? They are just like humans in that respect they will always take the easiest route, if there is a path, they'll use it.' said George.

'Fascinating.' replied Robert.

'I'll show you fascinating soon enough.' said Charles looking at the scene with a smile on his face.

The party were surrounding the scene from the edge of the miniature meadow. It was like a little den, with a fallen tree acting like a back wall, against the dense jungle. The guide looked at the four men with a concerned look on his face.

'It has been back.'

'When?' said Charles startled.

'Within the hour?' said the guide. 'Look at the pugmark.'

In a little clearing of loose dust was a large pug mark.

'By Jove, you're right.' said Charles. 'I'd say under an hour old sport they are fresh.'

'It is most curious, but back where you took the shot, there were some fresh tracks but I couldn't be sure that it was a tiger.' said the guide down on one knee in the vegetation.

'But it could have been?' asked Gerald.

'Easily.' said the Guide.

'So why didn't you ask me?' demanded Charles hotly.

'Don't know, sorry sir I guess I didn't want to be wrong.'

'Well don't think that again, confounded idiot, this thing is huge, possibly the largest cat ever seen, and I do not want to miss out on it, do you understand?'

The guide put his head down slightly as if to show submission, 'apologies it won't happen again.'

Suddenly a loud shot rang out.

The party all looked at each other for a second in a state of mumchance.

'*The Rolls.*' cried Charles, they all started running through the grass as fast they could. Charles led the pack, the guide was right behind him. The tall grass whipped their trousers as they raced through it.

George and Gerald watched as Charles and the guide disappeared into the verdant undergrowth and then Robert watched as George and Gerald did the same.

Robert pulled his gun out of the holster and continued running at full speed trying to catch up to the others, he was soon under the dark canopy and smashing his way through leaves that was almost as big as him, his foot hit something hard and he went flying through the air, landing in the dirt. He got up and realised he had dropped his gun.

Charles maintained the lead as he emerged from the canopy and the sunlight hit his face full on, he was temporarily blinded, when his sight was restored what he saw stopped him in his tracks.

He stood there dumbfounded at the scene that lay before him, the guide popped out of the jungle next and as they walked slowly forward Gerald and George joined them too.

'Good God!' said George. 'It can't be.'

'I'm afraid it is.' said the Guide.

There laying half on the ground with his back resting on the side of the *Rolls Royce Silver Ghost* was the driver, he was dead. His throat had been ripped out.

'Who has committed this travesty, he will hang by sunset, I swear it.' said Gerald pulling out his revolver and scanning the area.

'It's not a who, but a what?' said Charles looking to the Guide for confirmation of his thoughts.

The guide nodded knowingly, 'It was a tiger.'

'No it was *the* Tiger I came here to hunt.' said Charles bitterly.

'You can't be sure of that.' said George, drinking some water for the shock had made his dry throat.

'The hypothesis would make sense, the fresh tracks indicate that a tiger came from yesterday's scene and headed this way, they are very territorial so it would be quite a coincidence if it was not the same creature.' said the Guide albeit somewhat reluctantly.

'It was him alright; I feel in it my bones, not that I need to,' he said walking around the back of the car and finding fresh pugmarks in the dirt, 'look at these pugmarks all the ones we have seen today have been from the same cat, look at the size of them, I have never seen pug marks so big. I fear you are right this cannot be co-incidence.' said Charles pulling the cork out of a whisky bottle and drinking a large gulp, 'this is no time for water.' he said.

'And look, why didn't it take any of the food that he had started getting out?' said George looking at the food parcels scattered on the floor during the mayhem.

'And why didn't he drag the body off, we all know how easily a tiger can carry off a man.' said the Guide

'It looks like we have a man-eater.' said Charles cocking his rifle.

'Don't be so ridiculous Charles,' said George. 'You know they only attack for food and rarely turn man eater even after they have killed two or even three people.'

'What about the gunshot it could have scared it off.' suggested the guide.

'It is plausible, plenty of men have shot at tigers and still had them come.' said Gerald stroking his chin, 'Plenty of my friends have been shikari's.'

'Well there is no point on us speculating, I want to see the beast a hunter's instinct tells me it is the mate that I seek.' said Charles eventually passing the bottle of whisky to George.

George took a swig as did Gerald and the Guide, the Guide then gave the bottle back to George. 'What about you Rob ... *Great Scott, Where is Robert?*' cried George.

'I thought he was with us, he must have fell behind.' said Gerald. They all looked at the dead driver, then back at each other and raced quickly back into the Jungle.

'*Robert, Robert, speak up old chap, where are you?*' shouted Charles trying desperately to hide his concern.

'*Robert, Robert.*' The party shouted his name many times, but their calls were greeted only by responses from chirping insects and birds.

They traced their steps back the way they had come, towards the clearing, but fanned out as they did.

'What on earth has happened to him?' said the guide, trudging through the thick foliage. He stopped in his tracks and bent down to the ground. 'Come quick I have found something. The party all ran over to him and looked to where the guide was pointing. There in the grass lay Robert's revolver.

Charles leant over and picked it up, it hasn't even been fired, they looked around and discovered that the leaves and branches ahead had been greatly disturbed, and very recently.

Charles checked his rifle, the others pulled out their hand guns again. Charles led as they followed the trail of carnage, they pushed aside some leaves and continued walking, after about thirty more seconds they came across another pervasive set of giant tropical leaves, they bludgeoned their way through and were greeted by a most unpleasant sight.

'*Noooooooo.*' exclaimed the Guide.

Gerald took off his hat, and putting it on his chest did the sign of the cross with his free hand.

Charles just stared with hatred. Fury and obsession burnt in his eyes like a furnace melting steel. Robert laid there in front of them, leaning against a fallen log with his throat ripped out.

'There is something quite odd about this.' said the guide.

'What sort of obtuse comment is that.' snapped George, nervously holding his gun and holding it tighter as each second passed.

'Let me explain, if you look carefully you will realise that he wasn't killed here, he was killed back there, the ferociousness indicates he probably died instantly, but that is not what is odd about all this.'

'Then what the bloody hell is, get to the point.' said Gerald.

'You can see that most of the blood is upon himself, why isn't it all over the ground? I should think that the tiger took one bite killing him instantly and without letting go of his grip dragged him here.

'But why?' asked George.

'When a tiger drags away his food,' the guide continued, 'he takes it to feed on or stores it for later, and I do not know what you gentlemen will make of this, but to me it seems almost as if he has been ...'

'Put on display.' said Charles finishing his sentence, in a morose tone.

'What do you mean put on display? You mean to say that a tiger killed a man and dragged him through jungle to put him up as a threat or something.' said Gerald with flushed cheeks.

'Or a promise.' added Charles.

'Well, yes.' answered the guide.

'*Preposterous*.' said George his cheeks now more florid than his hair. 'It is an animal that is all.'

'Do not be so quick to judge an animal as having no intent.' said Charles looking gravely at the guide.

'*The Tsavo Man-Eaters*.' said the guide solemnly.

'Precisely.' said Charles.

'What on earth are the *Tsavo Man-Eaters* Charles?' said Gerald

'Two lions that kept attacking and eating people in Kenya. It is reckoned they killed over a hundred people, the pair of them kept on sneaking into a camp and taking people even after they had built defences.' said Charles without looking away from Robert's lifeless body.

'Yes that's right Charles, it was during construction of the railway, the thing is, it has been surmised that they killed for fun, for they killed more than they needed to eat.' said the Guide.

'That's Incredulous.' said George indignantly.

'That story is true, my friend was there.' said the guide.

'Revenge.' said Charles.

'What do you mean revenge man, tigers don't seek revenge.' implored Gerald.

'I was thinking out loud. Tell me Gerald what if someone killed the love of your life?' said Charles still staring at the body in front of him.

'It's a bloody beast and that is that.' said George with an emphatic finality.

'Look at the way the body is placed against the tree, *that is a pose.*' said Charles. They all looked at it and blood ran down their spine.

'Poor Robert,' said George.

'Yes, we must get him home.' said Gerald.

'Home, home, I assure you I am not going home, this beast thinks it can lay the gauntlet down on me, I swear his blood will be mine before I ever return home.' Charles screamed in a violent rage, his forehead and cheeks fighting for the strongest redness.

'Charles you not thinking straight, pull yourself together man.' shouted Gerald with equal temperament.

'We should not have come on this trip in the first place, you had your victory and we should have all left it there, it was man who envoked this, no one else.' George said, mopping his brow out of frustration more than necessity.

Before anyone could respond, the guide spoke up.

'Well, we need to get the body back to the *Rolls* first.'

Charles was still fuming, his eyes misted and his behaviour looked unpredictable.

'We'll carry a limb each.' said Charles approaching the body in a matter of fact way.

Charles grabbed the arm but when Gerald grabbed the other one he could not look at Robert for too long, for fear of showing emotion. The other two grabbed the legs and they all trudged slowly back to the car.

The sun was beating down on them mercilessly as they slung Robert's body into the foot well of the rear seat that already contained the manservant.

Charles picked the bottle of whisky up off the grass that had been hastily discarded when they made for the jungle, he took a large swig and gritted his teeth.

'Charles you must see sense and return with us, if you like, we can come back with twenty men and hunt this thing down, but not now, you are not thinking straight.'

'No, but I am aiming straight.' said Charles.

'Not if you keep drinking that you're not.' said George taking the bottle out of his hand and taking a drink himself.

'If you feel so strongly about it gentlemen, return and then come back with help but I assure you will find me deep in the hunt.' Charles said in an eerily quiet tone.

'Stop being so bloody minded Charles.' remonstrated Gerald.

'Bloody minded, bloody minded, I am man, I am the highest on the food chain and I will kill any creature, whether it be feathered, fur, scale or insect.' Charles was shaking his fists furiously.

Full of malice and rage Charles' red, blood-shot eyes stained with insanity turned and faced the jungle. He threw out his arms in a challenge like gesture to the animal kingdom. *'My house is filled with your skulls and hide, your insolence I will never abide.'*

Gerald stepped forward and as Charles turned back around Gerald grabbed him by his loose fitting shirt and shook him violently. 'Pull yourself together man what is wrong with you, we have lost two men for God's sake, we must regroup and do this properly.'

Charles just looked through him, 'It is no use my friend, leave me, I must finish this.'

'*Good God!*' cried George, the whisky bottle fell out of his hand to the ground, smashing on impact as it hit a small rock in the grass. George's face was a picture of horror and surprise, his eyes transfixed in amazement.

Charles, Gerald and the Guide instantly turned to see what had provoked this most remarkable reaction, and all their faces contorted with horror. The exception was Charles whose face grew redder than a crimson sun, for up ahead sitting on the stretch of grass that separated the jungle and the road was a huge male tiger, with a large gash in one of its front legs and fresh blood around its mouth.

It was just sitting there, impertinently watching their every move and swishing its tail back and forth.

Charles pulled up his rifle at record speed and let off a shot, the others all pulled out their revolvers and started firing as well. The tiger immediately ran at full speed with tree splinters dancing all around as it disappeared back into the jungle.

'You were right Charles, the thing has been maddened by some vengeful lust.' said Gerald.

'The way it looked at us.' said George trying to lift the whisky bottle to his lips but realising it was no longer there.

'This damn thing slowed me down.' said Charles violently removing his gun belt and throwing it into the back of the *Silver Ghost*, he re-loaded his rifle and started to walk toward the jungle.

'Charles if you must go, take some extra ammo.' said Gerald.

'Yes and some water.' added George returning to his senses.

Charles stopped in his tracks and returned to the party. 'Very well, I thank you and apologise for my behaviour, but do not try and stop me as my course will not be altered.'

'We can see that old chap.' said Gerald slapping him on his upper arm. Charles did not react, despite this strategic attempt to bring the man back round to reason, vexation still painted his face the colour of beetroot.

Gerald started throwing him some boxes of ammo which Charles stuffed in his pockets, one in each side of his trousers and on one in his breast pocket. 'Take your belt as well in case you need the revolver.'

'I don't need it Gerald, I am faster and better with this it was only because of that damned belt that I missed.'

'Well take this Charles.' said George handing him a large round canteen of water with a long strap attached. Charles placed the strap over his head and across his shoulders.

'I only wish that I had bought my 450 with me, a bit more stopping power.' said Charles.

'Yes but a lot heavier to carry, we still do not think it a wise option what you are doing but we understand it is something you feel you must do.'

'Thank you both, I appreciate your concern, but I will be quite alright, I tell you on this day any animal that crosses my path goes on my wall culminating with that infernal creature that dares to test me.'

'We will go straight back and raise the alarm, then we'll gather up some men and come straight back.'

'I will come with you Sir.' said the Guide.

'If you like, but don't hit that tiger, he is mine and only mine, understand?' required Charles throwing the guide a dead stare.

'I understand Sir, I will just help you track that is all.'

Charles said no more and started to walk off into the jungle. Gerald threw the guide a fresh canteen of water and he then followed a little way after him.

'Upon his safe return your pay will be doubled for the whole week.' shouted Gerald after him. The guide turned around and after nodding his understanding he turned back to follow Charles.

Charles' face was growing red again and although the madness in his eyes had seemed to dissipate slightly, it had now returned with a most fervent gaze. He did not even hear the car start up, such was the concentration on hunting his target.

Charles went about half way to where the clearing was and then cut through the jungle alongside the road to where the tiger had headed in. He was hoping it had ran into the jungle and then stopped, if that was the case he could come at it from the side and ambush it.

The guide caught up with him.

'Sir, we should head into that clear area and circumvent the periphery that way we can look for tracks to see where he has come out of the jungle and back in.'

'If he has? The cunning beast might have just ran for cover and then stayed put.'

'Even if he has we will know that and it will be easy to pick up his trail from our point of reference, and besides he will be expecting us from the road if that is where he is.'

Charles stopped for a second, and rubbed his chin. 'That makes sense, we should be able to get a definite idea of his bearing, and the sooner I bleed this adversary, the better. You *will* be paid double I will see to it.'

'Thank you sir.'

They changed course and headed back to the clearing via the old route, they followed their old footsteps and walked past the point where they had found Robert's gun and at last they came to the clearing.

As they came out into the clearing both men stopped dead in their tracks. Across the other side of the plain sitting where Charles had killed the female was the giant Male Tiger with the wound on its leg. It just sat there looking at them, waiting as if the rendezvous had been pre-arranged.

'Before the guide could even speak Charles let off a shot with his rifle, but the tiger anticipated it jumping over the log and into the jungle with perfect timing.'

'You are a quick shot.' said the guide.

'Evidently not quick enough, come on let's get this beast.'

The pair started running across the plain but stopped short to catch their breath.

'Let us split up.' said Charles.

'Do you think that is wise?'

Charles looked at the guide's worried face. 'Not far, let us go into the Jungle but keep within sight of each other, that way he has less chance of escaping our sight.'

'Perhaps, we just wait for some more men; this tiger appears to be toying with us.'

'Nonsense, he is just a dumb, but particularly brave animal, but not for much longer I assure you. All he is doing is dancing with his own fate, but shoot near him not at him, remember this kill is mine.'

'Very well,' said the guide pulling the gun out of his holster. The guide went to the side about twenty paces and entered the jungle. Charles went straight through the spot where the tiger had been sitting and stepped over the fallen log into the dense undergrowth.

There was a lot of excitement in the Jungle, Red Monkey's were squealing, Chital Deer were barking, birds were flapping and insects clacking. 'The tiger must be nearby' Charles thought to himself.

'Careful old boy, I don't think he is far.' Charles said looking to his side just about making out the guide's figure proceeding forward. The guide gave him a thumbs up.

Charles continued with his rifle at the ready, looking around him with every step. His obsession with finding this creature swelled, fear never entered his mind, looking this way and that, he stepped ever deeper into the jungle.

Prudence eventually got the better of him, he thought it might be wiser to re-group with the guide or at least get closer as the tiger wasn't being flushed out, they would need to resort back to tracking.

He shouted the guide loudly, but there was no response. He shouted again, this time much louder. Charles didn't understand for he had been careful to keep looking in the guide's direction in order to check that he was still there, he headed over to where he had seen him less than a minute ago.

He stood there baffled but alert, then he saw the breakage in the grass and the leaves, it looked like something had been dragged through it, Charles gritted his teeth and then finally let out a blood curdling scream that echoed through the jungle.

Charles was hyperventilating he put his head down and lifted it up with ferocity screaming into the jungle,

'Where are you wretched, infernal, beast?'

He decided to follow the drag marks so he could find the guide's body, but the sound of a twig snapping distracted him and as he swung round he saw the tiger looking at him, its bloody mouth appeared to be smiling.

The Tiger was close enough for a decent shot but Charles was so enraged that he charged after it before he had even brought up his rifle. He hastily brought the rifle up for a shot as he ran. He fired and missed, then he fired again and missed. Charles then halted and took aim but the tiger changed direction and disappeared into some heavy shrubbery. 'Infernal Beast.' he said to himself stalking through the jungle after his prey.

He stopped to look for tracks and momentarily realised that he was alone, in the middle of the jungle. He quickly put the thought out of his mind, rapidly imagining capturing his quarry and returning to the hotel in great triumph with its huge carcass slung over his shoulder.

He surveyed the area carefully but he could not tell what way to go next. Then as he looked up he saw in the distance the familiar bloodied face looking backing at him. The Tiger ran as soon as he looked and Charles gave chase stopping a few minutes later to gather his bearings, but determined the tiger would tire before him.

The swig of water was refreshing and after screwing the canteen lid back on, he waited. A commotion caught his attention, something large was moving through the undergrowth at rapid speed. The tiger was quite near and sprinting straight across his line of vision. It went through some trees and disappeared into some thick scrub.

Charles again gave chase but the creature had moved at such velocity that Charles decided not to waste a shot. He could not stop himself from wondering what the tiger was up to, perhaps he was finally wearing it down and maybe it was starting to grow tired, panicking as it could not lose its relentless pursuer.

Charles walked through the foliage and some large trees then barged his way defiantly through the bush, he emerged out of the Jungle.

He came out onto a stretch of grass that led to a large river, a trail led to an old rope bridge that crossed the wide torrent. Charles knew where he was, there was a village about five miles downstream.

The tiger was nowhere to be seen. He walked towards the long narrow rope bridge, his rifle primed in a firing position. Just before the bridge was a large patch of wet mud with a puddle in the middle of it. Leading away from it, straight across the wooden boards of the rope bridge were the unmistakable paw prints of the large male tiger.

Carrying his rifle more casually and setting off across the rope bridge Charles sniggered to himself, 'as I said just a stupid animal.' The bridge wasn't particularly high the water was about ten or twelve feet below but the river was quite wide. He stopped a quarter of the way across to check the landscape on the other side, thinking if he could shoot it while taking a shot from a wobbling rope bridge, it would be a bonus to his double trophy.

With no sign of the male tiger he carried on crossing the bridge, but was stopped by this overwhelming sense that he was being watched. He turned around to look back the way he had come and was horrified to see the tiger he had been watching him, standing there but this time with a vicious snarl.

Charles was about to try and bring up his rifle convinced the tiger was going to charge him on the bridge, but instead the tiger swiped the ropes with his huge claws cutting the bridge. Charles was immediately emptied into the water, during his fall his gun was thrown into the river as he tried hopelessly to grab hold of something.

Immediately coming to his senses in the river, he looked frantically for his gun, but it was no use, the water was deep and he had no hope of finding it. He needed to get out of the water quick. The shore he left was still the nearer and he swam straight for it. Upon reaching it he desperately pulled himself up onto the muddy bank.

The bank went up onto a lip of earth and he saw the Tiger towering above him, looking larger than ever. It just stood there growling. Charles looked behind thinking he would have to try and swim back across. Fear finally took hold of him as he turned around to see several large fully grown crocodiles swimming in towards him.

In desperation he turned and looked back at the bank, the Tiger leant in and downwards closer to Charles. The pads of its front feet were placed right on the edge of the bank, so the tiger could dangle all of its razor sharp claws over the edge, they shone like kitchen knives in the sunlight. Its eyes were full of bloodthirsty revenge and snarling viciously with all his teeth exposed, the tiger licked his lips.

Tiger! Tiger! Tiger!

Volume II

The Fallen and the Missing

The old colonial palace now serving as a hotel stood brusquely in juxtaposition to the surrounding jungle akin to an iceberg on an English summer meadow. The sabre shaped, sunlit neon leaves surrounded it like a swarm of Arabic swords.

The black and white chequered tiles of the bar floor still stood in proud opposition to the wicker furniture, the same mixologist patiently awaited custom, the fans whirred still ruffling the exotic plants, everything seemed as before, albeit the colonel and his wife were absent.

The room however, felt empty, as if something was off kilter, the mysterious miasma of despair hung in the air like an unwelcome aroma.

Four men sat round the same table as Charles' had just two days previous. Concerned looks addressed their faces, a bottle of brandy sat on the table and all the men had brandy glasses in front of them, except for Gerald who had his in his hand.

George's face looked awash with perplexity as if some great burden should be about to fall upon him. His gingerish red hair was slightly more unkempt than usual but not enough for him to be described as scruffy. His cotton shirt was taut from the muscular mass that was seeking freedom.

The guide sat there looking down at the glass on the table, his expression was forlorn and his clear shaved skin seemed painted with worry. His neatly styled black hair caught the natural light giving it a sheen that marked him out for special attention.

The fourth man was tall with heavy set curly black hair. His dress was slightly different than the others, he wore trousers and a shirt suitable more for London than the heart of the Indian jungle. The dark green shirt that despite its colour looked more smart than casual, his trousers were black and the material appeared thick, the black military style boots tried poorly to disguise themselves as shoes.

'To the fallen and the missing.' said Gerald raising his Brandy glass.

The others all raised their glasses.

'To Charles, may he be well.' said George.

'To the driver.' said the guide.

'To Robert.' said the fourth man.

The four men all took big gulps of the liquor and returned their glasses to the table and sat back.

'You know I never actually met Robert although I have heard good things, the poor man.'

'It is sadness beyond comprehension that he should die in such a way, but it was Charles who knew him well. Gerald and I were acquaintances albeit we liked him.' said George.

Gerald nodded his approval to George's comment.

'So what the devil has happened to Charles? I venture southwards for a few weeks and calamity strikes, most singular indeed.' said the fourth man.

'Singular and tragic.' echoed George.

'I hope he is still alive.' said the guide.

'Worry presses me, albeit I cannot help but think that he is as strong as an ox and as stubborn as that tiger.' Gerald said picking his glass up.

'His stubbornness could be the problem.' said George.

'He could be alive, he could be dead, we do not know and therefore cannot speculate.' said the fourth man.

'No, I think we can speculate, after all we do know the man. If he has not returned within forty eight hours I will not find it as easy to hope I tell you that.' said George.

'That's why we must find him before then.' said Gerald removing his panama hat revealing sweaty black hair that now looked akin to a nest.

'Absolutely.' said the guide.

'So what exactly happened out there?' said the fourth man helping himself to a refill.

'You have already been told, for the most part, last night. We all embarked on a tiger hunt and somehow the tiger turned the tables.' said George.

'I am not sure that is an apt description old boy, my account would asseverate the retelling of a beast who got lucky a couple of times. We should have all returned to the hotel, to continue after tragedy has struck is always a bad omen; if not a supernatural one, certainly a logical one.' said Gerald.

'The reason for our tryst here today is so we ourselves can understand what happened, form a plan and know how the guide managed to return.' said George sitting up in his chair.

'Yes and how he came back without incident.' added Gerald looking at the guide with quizzical eyes.

'Sounds like you have some explaining to do my fellow.' The fourth man said with a glint of seriousness crossing his face.

'Forgive me sir but we have not been properly introduced.' said the guide in reply.

'Confound it, this awful mess has my mind agog with preoccupation, I forget the most simple things. This is Alistair, a much trusted friend and companion and Alistair this is our guide, his family is well known around these parts.' said George motioning his hands between them.

Alistair looked at the guide studiously, 'And what is your real name? You must have one.'

'I do, it is just no one ever asks.' George cleared his throat. 'Except for George that is. My name is Inderjhit, but people call me Inda.'

Gerald shuffled awkwardly in his seat at this revelation. 'Yes well sorry old chap I never thought to ask, simple oversight I assure you, so do tell us what happened when you and Charles left myself and George.'

Inda resigned himself from further social effort and took a sip of his Brandy, after returning it to the wicker and glass coffee table he rubbed his face and looked up at the three men.

'There is not much to tell I am afraid gentlemen, after you left we tracked the tiger successfully, came across the clearing and found the male tiger in the spot where Charles had shot its mate. Charles immediately let off a shot but missed, we dashed across the meadow in pursuit. When we reached the jungle Charles insisted that we split up, of course I remonstrated with him that it was a foolish option but he would not have any of it and I was forced to walk into the Jungle several hundred yards away from him. It was during that time that I lost him.'

'Come, come, Inda you do not tell us all, for we know about the drag marks with no blood. Charles tracked you and upon finding the drag trail assumed what you had planned him to assume didn't he?' said Gerald sitting bolt right up in his chair.

Inda hung his head downwards, 'yes it is as you say, I tell you in all my years as a tracker never has fear filled me like that, it visited me like a foreseer of death and I cowered, I had no choice, my body could do only one thing and that was survive. I knew that all hope was lost, I was to die so I panicked and clumsily dragged myself through the jungle floor creating as much disturbance as I could, then I fled. I tell you the truth even after I had made my escape I did not expect to live; I thought the feline spectre of vengeance would surely chance upon me.'

'But it did not.' said Alistair looking stern.

'No, it did not sir.' said Inda meeting his stare; it was only when I got home that I felt the full force of my guilt. As some of you will be aware my family are held in high regard by the British and we have served you as trackers for generations. It was my father's reputation which enabled me to study at Oxford, but when I shared with him my disgrace, he scolded me and beat me even though I am a fully grown man.'

Inda suddenly burst out into tears, he cried vigorously but only for a short spell and then he composed himself as best he could. 'Please excuse me gentlemen I do not know what has come over me.'

'Yes well, pull yourself together there's a good chap.' said George leaning forward across the table and pushing Inda's brandy glass toward him.

Inda looked deeply into the glass, a solitary tear betrayed him and dropped into the brandy with a splash that seemed amplified by the atmosphere. 'I know I am a coward, a cur as you would say, I know I ran, that I turned on my tails but I assure you it is worse than you can ever know, we Indian people are proud and I have disgraced my family, I must assuage the dishonour and pursue my tormentor.'

'Come, come Inda there is no requirement for such melodrama, we can see you're penitent.' said George.

'Yes even I shall agree to that.' said Alistair taking a large gulp of his Brandy.

'So that is all there is to tell about what happened to Charles?' asked Gerald.

'Yes, that was the last I saw of him, but I have already sought to make reparations.' Inda replied sitting back.

'What do you mean?' asked Alistair.

'I have asked every tracker in the region to look for him and the cat, we are swarming the entire area, it is a matter of family honour so there are no shortage of volunteers. I expect it will not be long before we know of the whereabouts of both Charles and our so called feline avenger.' Inda said sighing heavily.

'What is it old man?' asked Gerald.

'It is just that I fear the worst, he must have been eaten or destroyed.' Inda said nervously taking another drink.

'He's probably barbecuing the bloody thing.' said George. The room erupted with loud laughter and for a moment the fog of despair lifted.

'We have no evidence that he isn't anything but fine.' Gerald said when the laughter had died and the eerie silence had returned.

'Why hasn't he contacted us then?' Inda replied.

'I am not saying do not worry, but we have no idea what is happening, albeit I think we need to get out there and look for him.' Gerald replied.

'There isn't a man here who wouldn't agree with that.' said Alistair.

'That is what I thought, I have drawn up a plan, I think it would be best if we start from where he was last seen, Inda, if you show us where that was, we'll try and track him from there.' said Gerald.

'Yes, there would be no reason for him to hide his tracks, but my men should have been on that already and they are competent trackers.' said Inda scratching his head.

'I'll bloody kill him myself when I get my hands on him.' said Gerald exhaling deeply, a slight quiver visible on his lips.

At that moment a man came through the door wearing kahki clothes, he looked fairly dirty and ruffled, he was a skinny Indian man of medium height, as he approached the table he took off his Khaki coloured hat and held it to his chest. He looked straight at Inda.

'Inda we must talk urgently I have news.'

Inda gulped. 'Hari, sit down and tell us, these are the gentlemen concerned.'

Hari took a seat but sat on the edge and maintained an upright posture.

'We have found Charles.'

'Where did you find him?' asked Alistair with furrowed eyebrows.

'They did not exactly find him I am afraid Sir.' replied Hari.

'What the bloody hell are you talking about either you found him or you didn't?' Alistair said, his cheeks flushing.

Hari nervously played with his hat. 'I mean parts of him were found at the river where the rope bridge crosses, some of the villagers stumbled across him. It seems as if he was cornered by both tiger and crocodile.' Hari looked down into his lap again as soon as he had said it.

'How ghastly.' added George looking solemnly into his glass.

'To Charles, the greatest hunter I ever met!' said Gerald picking his brandy glass off of the table and raising it.

'Charles.' toasted George solemnly.

'Charle …' Inda spluttered his face filling with moisture. Emotion and determination fought vigorously across the canvas of his face as he wrestled back his untimely outburst. 'Charles.' He said again with an over compensatory thrust of his arm.

'Our friend and compatriot.' said Alistair raising his glass not quite as high as the others but with a melancholic lift.

'So what is your plan?' asked George.

'The plan is simple, find that blasted tiger and kill it.' said Gerald leaning forward and refilling everyone's glasses.

'Absolutely sir. I have some of the best men I know awaiting my word, as soon as I give it they will assist us in the hunt and that it is not all Gentlemen, we have more ingenuity than you might give us credit for – I have already requested that traps be laid in likely sites.'

'With the greatest of respect Inda you say that you have some of your best men waiting – Charles was the probably the best hunter in the British Empire.' said George with a slightly florid face.

'His point has merit.' said Alistair looking thoughtful.

'Nonsense, it got lucky I do not know how, but it did, we shall find it and kill it and then let our friend rest.' said Gerald.

'Here, here.' toasted Alistair.

'It seems to me that we are just going to do the same thing we did last time and what if we have the same result?' said George sitting back in the chair with his refilled brandy glass in hand.

'Apologies George but I must agree with Gerald what happened before was highly irregular, it is a bloody cat, that is all and we shall end its life whether it likes it or not, it has killed one of us so it must die, end of.' said Alistair.

'Yes George, we will hunt easily enough you shall see, we have the guide and he has a lot of people out there assisting, we shall take more men with us this time.' Gerald said leaning forward slightly.

'Charles was worth ten men with a rifle and you both know it.' said George.

'What the bloody hell is wrong with you man, it's a cat that is all, it wants a war, we'll give it one.' Gerald said returning his panama hat onto his head.

George fidgeted in his chair his cheeks flushing crimson red. 'I have a lost a dear friend, something's not right about this whole affair but do not bring some twisted malevolence in to this, we hunted it in the first place, we killed its mate, it is not as if it randomly started attacking.'

'Are you a hunter or not? If you do not have stomach for danger then just say.' said Alistair.

Gerald clapped his hand to his forehead and looked down.

'Who do you address sir? You dare speak to me about courage, you bloody ignoramus, I will you show you courage.' said George putting down his glass and leaping out of his chair.

Gerald reached out his hand, grabbed George's forearm and looked at him. George exhaled deeply and sat back down.

'I apologise George, you are a formidable opponent I know, but I do not understand your behaviour, as much as I count you as my friend there is conflict within you about all this, of that I am sure.'

'Listen, I shall accompany you if you decide to track this tiger, but I would rather the tiger lived and my friends remain intact than the tiger dies and we lose even one soul.'

'I understand your concern George, but I am going to kill that bloody cat and that is all there is to it, it can't win again, it is just a beast that is all. Why you are so worried? We know of your war history and battlefield experience, you're fearless. You have seen combat like no other and reportedly kept your composure throughout and hitherto come to that, but that is what perplexes me, what is really bothering you old man?' said Gerald looking contemplatively at his friend, his thick black eyebrows accentuating the point.

'There is something peculiar about this whole affair, I have an extraordinarily bad feeling. I tell you, regardless of any emotion, my instinct says we should leave this matter be.'

'Confound you George you are talking out of sorts now – since when do you talk about gut feelings?' cried Gerald

'Indeed I haven't, not since the war anyway.' said George.

'Confounded botheration, this mess has you all churned up and spun round, in a couple of days you will see, reason will prevail you will see.' said Alistair swirling his drink round in his glass.

'I hope you are right.' George said still confident in his previous statement.

'I must say sir I did share your sentiment, but I have no choice now, that tiger has shamed me, it made me fearful and for that he will pay. I will avenge my master.'

'You sound like a rabid dog Inda.' said George.

'George leave it be, he is right, regardless of what you think.' said Alistair.

'I shall come with you, if we get a location on this tiger I shall have your back, but if tragedy strikes but once, I will return as I am not prepared to stroll on in a climate of madness. I tell you straight gentlemen, Gerald, both you and Inda are full of foolish revenge and obsession, as we said to Charles no good can come of it. I can see it in your eyes so don't take me for a bloody fool, and as for you Alistair you seem to be needlessly stirring the pot, I will warn you not to stir me too much my friend.'

'You have made your feelings clear George; I hear your point but we are all our own men here and we will do as we wish.' Alistair retorted with some anger but also a slight laden of fear.

'George I warmly appreciate your assistance on any undertaking that we embark upon, I respect your opinion immensely, perhaps you have said some truths, we are full of mixed emotions and the Brandy riles us. I say to you George that if calamity should fall upon us we shall turn back at once.'

'That is an offer my friend that I accept gladly.' said George extending his hand. Gerald took it and after placing his other hand on the top shook it firmly.

'Some of our exchanges tonight have been regrettable, I also apologise.' said Alistair lifting his glass at George.

'We are all out of sorts.' said George rising his glass with a slight smile at Alistair.

'What shall we do if we do not hear anything within the next couple of days?' said George looking at Inda.

'We will hear before the day is out, I will stake my reputation on it … well maybe not my reputation now.' This bought a cacophony of laughter from George, Gerald and Alistair. Inda found himself chuckling along with them.

'Inda, you are a funny man.' said Alistair.

'Inda, Inda, Inda, Inda …' The glass doors flew open with a loud slam, the glass shook violently and nearly broke, a man sporting a turban and camouflaged clothing ran into the bar still shouting *'Inda, Inda, Inda, Inda.'*

'What in the blasted wretchedness is all this commotion?' said Gerald standing up and looking around.

The man who had ran into the bar immediately spotted them and headed over.

'Inda, Inda we have spotted it, the tiger we have spotted it, we have spotted it.'

'Well pull up a chair and tell us, what do you mean bursting in here causing such a blasted ruckus, master your emotions man.' shouted Gerald.

'Sorry sir.' said the man getting a chair from another table and joining them.

'Barman another glass please.' said George standing up and clicking his fingers. George sat back down.

'This is my friend Vijay, he has been helping us with the tracking of the tiger.' said Inda

'Sorry for my outburst but I am very excited to tell you that we have spotted your cat.' said Vijay

'See, what did I tell you Gentlemen, I told you we would hear today.' Inda exclaimed, some life returning to him as he said it.

There was a clink as the barman put a spare glass on the table. George immediately filled it with Brandy and handed it to Vijay.

'Take a deep breath, have a drink and then calmly tell us every detail.' said Alistair. Vijay did as he was told, he took a deep breath, then a large sip but choked on it slightly. Gerald rolled his eyes.

'It has been spotted a few miles out only a ten minute drive in the car.' said Vijay.

'Ten minutes?' asked Inda.

'But that means it is getting closer.' said George.

'The thing must be stupid.' Alistair said ruffling his curly black hair.

'Most peculiar, why the hell would it come closer?' said Gerald swigging down a large gulp.

'That's what worries me,' said George stroking his chin.

'That's not all.' said Vijay. 'The group of men who saw it were building a large trap, they were nearly finished when the tiger leapt out of the Jungle and stood on the track right in front of them, almost as if it was challenging them. They said the cat just sat there swishing its tail looking at them.'

'What happened next?' said Gerald.

'They just stood there and stared in not belief …'

'Disbelief.' Inda corrected.

'… In disbelief, they were too scared to even try and fight, they said that the tiger just kept sitting there staring at them, they grabbed their tools, their guns and slowly walked backwards until the tiger was out of view.'

'Confound them all, what did they do that for?' said Alistair.

'Because it was only thing they dared do, they say that particular cat is not an animal but an angry spirit sent to avenge and punish.' said Vijay nervously taking another sip of his drink.

'What utter nonsense.' said Gerald.

George sat silent and sipped his drink while slowly rubbing his chin.

'Well it has crossed the line for the last time.' said Gerald, sitting straight up in his seat.

'Yes Gerald, you are quite right. Vijay, rally some men, get the *Silver Ghost's* and meet us outside in twenty minutes.' said Inda, acting assertive for the first time since the beginning of their inter-locution.

'Yes the time has come, let us arm ourselves and kill this beast once and for all.' said Alistair taking a large gulp of the brandy.

'Are you still with us George?' asked Gerald.

'As I said I am with you until tragedy strikes then you shall all follow me in returning, if you don't, then upon your head be it.' he replied sitting forward in a confident fashion.

The three men all looked at each other and nodded.

'Then why do we wait?' said George.

'That's more like it.' said Gerald slapping his friend hard on the back.

'Outstanding.' said Alistair gulping back a big swig of brandy upon which he almost choked.

'At last my name shall be restored.' said Inda with satisfaction.

'Let us go with strong heart and immense courage.' said George lifting his glass.

The three men toasted but this time without call.

'Then let us prepare.' said George, standing up.

'Shall we say, outside in ten?' said Alistair.

'That will suffice.' replied George.

The men separated, George went back to his camp, Alistair returned to his motor vehicle, Gerald went to the bar for he kept his hunting equipment on site at the hotel.

Ten minutes later, what looked like preparation for a military invasion assembled outside. Two dark green, customised and fortified *Rolls Royce Silver Ghost's* each with their own driver, fully equipped with supplies, extra seating and storage stood alongside George, Gerald, Inda and Alistair. All of whom were adorned in full hunting gear, including hunting knives, revolvers, rifles, pith helmets and khaki uniforms.

'Have you seen George's rifle? The 450, that is a powerful, accurate shot, I dream that I should I own such a thing.' said Inda mesmerised.

'He is not a man to be underestimated.' said Gerald whispering into his ear.

'I am starting to see that.' replied Inda.

The vehicles, identical to the ones that they had left in with Charles the day before, stood in symmetrical alignment awaiting embarkation.

The men climbed aboard the first car, including Vijay who had also armed himself appropriately. Aboard the second *Rolls Royce* were six men all armed with rifles and dressed in beige uniform, stocks and supplies hung precariously off the back of both cars.

'The men in the other vehicle are all experienced hunters and trackers, we are in safe hands.' said Inda from the passenger seat.

'Time will foretell that my friend.' said George from the back.

'You are right on that my compatriot but I have a good feeling about this, you will see, we shall return triumphant victorious.' said Gerald allowing a smile to shine from his face.

'Yes he is right George, you shall see, we will all laugh about our preposterous deliberations tonight I assure you.' said Alistair slapping George on his shoulder.

The *Silver Ghost* rumbled down a dirt track, the men swayed and bumped as if in some synchronised dance. Spirits were high and the drink still flowed albeit they had now switched to whisky. In the second vehicle the men were silent, melancholic, thoughtful even, as if they were about to enter some great battlefield each man had his own thoughts, his own prayers as they solemnly bumped their way along the road.

It was not long before they reached their destination, for too many of the slightly inebriated men in the front vehicle it felt like they had just pulled off when they arrived.

'It is a fifteen minute walk to the site of the trap from here, I suggest that we prepare for a long trek anyway.' said Vijay.

'He is right gentlemen, we should prepare as if we are hiking in the jungle for a day or two just in case.' said Inda.

'Now the man talk's sense.' said George energetically leaping from the car.

Specially designed ration packs, water bottles, and a first aid kit, which included anti-venom for the array of poisonous snakes and insects were handed out.

The men from both cars alighted and congregated like a garrison, with guns, rifles and knives showing in all directions, man and his tools of war shone brazenly in the hot Indian sun.

They prepared themselves giving each other nods of bravery and approval.

'Listen here my friends.' said Inda addressing Vijay and the accompanying men who had travelled in the second vehicle.

'We are here to kill the huge male tiger that has a large open scar down its left leg to its foot. You will not break away unless requested to and you shall not try and take the beast alone, if Gerald, George, Alistair or myself want the shot then you will submit, do you understand?'

'Yes,' they all said in unison holding their rifles slightly in salute as they did.

'In fact,' said George stepping forward, 'the drivers can return with the vehicles back to the hotel but you are to return to this spot every two hours unless instructed otherwise by one of us four.'

The two drivers who were wearing smart clothes bowed their heads slightly and returned to the *Silver Ghost's*, dust kicked up as they turned the vehicles around and headed off down the dirt track back toward the hotel.

The men gathered in a rough circle. 'Inda and myself shall take point with George and Alistair directly behind. We shall trek in two's where the track allows and single file where it doesn't. Inda, your men are to follow behind and to fan out in an amiable fashion where ever possible to cover all the angles, we must be vigilant, everyone must be accounted for at all times. If you are in doubt, if you even suspect something is amiss do not hesitate to speak up. I promise you that you will not be remonstrated for it.' said Gerald.

Inda and his men all nodded.

'There is eleven of us in all, that should be plenty as long as we do not act like fools, this tiger is nothing but a large cat and we shall have no problem in slaying it, do you understand?'

'Yes Sir.' came the reply from the six hunters and trackers brought to assist.

'Troop, forward march.' shouted George in a voice so commanding that it even startled Gerald.

They headed into the jungle, Inda leading the way with his Machete out ready to cut a path when they needed to.

The Jungle was thick, hot, large leaves slapped and stung their faces like frenzied wasps. Their comfy boots and hunting wear soon became their torturer, sweat rashes and bites set in, but they ploughed on in silence, it was only supposed to be a short walk but it ended up taking hours.

They reached the spot where the tiger had last been seen, feeling like they had just marched two days without supplies; the liquor began to betray the four leading men as headaches and fatigue started to pester. The whisky was handed around and each man gulped more than a civil amount in order to keep their strength what it was.

The track had widened enough to even let a vehicle through it.

'Is this the place Vijay?'

Vijay stepped forward from the head of his six companions and looked. 'Yes this is it, the trap is just ahead be very careful, it is large.' he said wiping the sweat from his forehead on his camouflaged clothing.

'Then lead the way old chap.' said George waving his hand.

'Very well.' said Vijay bowing slightly and slowly walking forward. He looked like a stealthy cat himself as he skulked forward watching every step, making certain he knew exactly where the tiger trap was, suddenly he threw his hand up and the whole party stopped.

'Look at the disturbance in the grass and leaves, this is where it starts, it covers the whole track, you must follow me into the trees so we can circumvent it.'

Vijay chopped his way into the thick jungle, they all followed as he carved a side path that came out a little further down the track.

'I must say you are good trap setters, I would not have seen it should I have not been looking for it.' said Alistair mopping his brow with a handkerchief.

The party congregated again on the other side.

'What now?' said Gerald.

'We are standing on the very place where we saw it.' said Vijay pointing at the ground.

'So now we track it.' said Inda.

'Then lead the way,' Alistair said.

Inda started to trek forward down the track, the temperature was stifling, heat lines quivered violently as if one were entering some dreamlike montage. George, Gerald and Alistair followed, with Vijay and the troop closely behind. They marched forward at a slow pace with Inda bending over following the animal's tracks diligently but cautiously. Determination burned in his eyes like some irremovable scar.

'Come on cat where are you, these tracks are fresh it should be close by ... aha, the sport commences.' said Inda turning around to his followers.

'Meaning?' said George.

Meaning that I am on its trail, it went into the Jungle over there, we must go in single file for the foliage is thick. Inda withdrew his machete and walked in a diagonal line into the jungle.

It was dense, the kaleidoscopic colours and shades felt somewhat disorientating, the humidity was so full that every breath of air competed with a myriad of overwhelming flower perfumes and plant secretions. Yet they all acted as if it was some genteel afternoon stroll they had embarked upon, no one dared be the first to complain of the conditions for fear that they would be thought of as a lesser man.

A twig snapped loudly and the men with Cobra like instincts cocked and pointed their guns. They all became somewhat more cautious after that.

'Do not forget what we are dealing with here.' said George.

'I won't and I am going to deal with it, that you can be assured of.' said Gerald. George rolled his eyes but Gerald did not see him.

Suddenly a large roar was heard nearby in the jungle, groups of Langur monkey's squawked and clattered through the trees sending leaf confetti, glittering down through the jungle canopy.

'Keep your nerve men, it is just trying to frighten us, it knows that we are on its trail.'

'*Blast*.' shouted Inda.

'What is it man?' asked Alistair.

'I have lost its track.'

'Confound you, you are supposed to be the best tracker in the region, how could you have lost him?' asked Gerald.

'I don't know, I tell you, it is like it has just disappeared.' said Inda shrugging his shoulders.

'It couldn't have just bloody disappeared Inda, it's a cat not a ghost ship.' said Alistair.

Inda turned and looked back at Vijay who had crept forward to survey the scene for himself, he looked back at Inda and shrugged his shoulders.

'Let us just keep moving forward, it can't be far.' said Gerald.

'If it is *the* cat that we heard.' said George taking a swig from a bottle of whisky and then passing it on.

'It is, I know it is.' said Gerald with bloodshot eyes. 'Only one of us will leave this jungle.'

'We will find our quarry and avenge my master that I promise.' said Inda taking hold of the whisky.

The men crept forward with guns at the ready, each step carefully monitored. Instinctively they began to keep a closer watch, every sound seemed amplified, noises that were not noticed before were suddenly heard, too many unfamiliar sounds, too many unfriendly whispers, heart rates started to rise, pulses triggered to a rapid beat.

They stopped, the track split into two, each path narrow and dark.

'What way?' Vijay whispered.

'What do you think Gerald?' said George.

'I don't know, we heard the tiger from that direction and from the looks of these paths they would go either side of where we heard the tiger, meaning …'

'… meaning if we went down both paths the tiger would be flushed out into one of us.'

'Exactly Inda, what do you think?'

'Certainly sounds plausible.' said Alistair pushing his way into the conversation.

'As long as the information is accurate then there is no reason why it shouldn't.' Inda said, bending over and closely examining the surrounding trees and bracken.

'And what happened to strength in numbers?' asked George.

'We will be fine George.' said Gerald placing his hand on George's sweaty shoulder.

'Confound your obstreperous ways Gerald I knew you would do this, you have always been of an obstinate disposition, but do not forget my words old man for I shall keep my promise, just one incident …'

'Yes okay George, but we need your help to go about this.' said Alistair.

George was put on the back foot by the compliment, he ran his eyes over the men and immediately started pointing his fingers. 'Inda select the five best men out of the six and instruct them to carefully take the path to the left, leave the man with the least experience with us.'

'Why the worst one we want the best, surely?' asked Alistair.

'We are all capable, they need the best chance we can give them, we have the extra man so we are still at an advantage, and besides, if anyone should try and kill this beast, you would all be cambering on top of them to get there first.' replied George.

'See, that it is why we want you here, you always make sense.' said Gerald.

George let out a loud laugh. 'I'm sorry, are you sure you're not confusing me with someone you listen to.'

The men all laughed briefly and passed around the bottle. George took out an unopened whisky bottle and gave it to Vijay. 'Give this to your men for luck and courage.' Vijay took it and had already selected the five men without mention from Inda for he had followed the conversation closely.

'Check yourselves gentlemen, we are about to bag us a trophy.' said Alistair. All the men re-checked their guns, knives and pistols and then the two parties separated and went down either trail. Inda again led their party followed by George, Gerald, Alistair, Vijay and the extra tracker.

The other party walked timidly through the Jungle, all were experienced hunters but they had heard the rumours about the cat that could not be slain who had been sent to punish man for his spiteful inequities. The most experienced man led the way, the pathway was a thin strip of dirt leading its way through the jungle like a trail of breadcrumbs.

Every sound had the men reacting with over-zealous strikes, even sounds familiar to them, they opened the whisky and drank as if it would somehow resolve all their problems, they proceeded on none the less.

All of a sudden there was a large commotion in the jungle, leaves parted and twigs broke, a flash, an image, a moment's reflection, something moved in the jungle, something was out there and active.

The jungle exploded with gunfire as the five men fired in all directions, shards of leaf and bark somersaulted through the air like a synchronised gymnastic team.

Back on the other trail ...

'Damn them, what is all that firing.' shouted George.

'We must go to them quick.' said Inda.

'*No, blast you man*, they are obviously firing at it and driving it this way like they are supposed to.' said Alistair

'*Get ready all, Inda forward slowly.*' said Gerald. The men all moved forward slowly with their weapons poised. Suddenly silence fell upon the jungle.

'Stop.' said George in a barely audible voice yet somehow they all heard and stopped.

Their hearts raced as they listened to the eerily silent jungle. They approached a small clearing.

'Something is not right I can feel it.' George continued, scanning the periphery, this time his comment met no argument, but something grew in his senses, there was something in the jungle, something that shouldn't be there, it was ... it was a sound, a faint but distinctive gurgling ...

'*What the hell is that noise*? Vijay control yourself man we are trying to listen.' snapped George.

'Sir it is not me, it mu …'

'*Great God.*' shouted Inda turning round.

'*Inconceivable.*' said Alistair his mouth hopelessly agape.

They all turned around and past them all, Inda, George, Gerald, Alistair and Vijay, the man at the back stood there with an irreparable amount of blood pumping from his throat. His eyes were wide, filled with horror and surprise, lacerated skin hung loose like red cabbage leaves, the blood sprayed, dripped, fell and poured in all directions. The man grabbed his throat but his hand was saturated in blood instantaneously, he fell to his knees and after giving a shallow nod to everyone he dropped dead.

'*Perimeter Quick.*' yelled George.

'*What?*' returned Alistair.

'*Set a blasted perimeter, Inda, you there, Alistair there, Vijay behind the body.*' Vijay hesitated.

'*If you want to live do as your bloody told.*' said George with flushed cheeks.

Vijay stepped over his friend's body trying not look and faced back into the jungle.

'*Good Gerald, you take that direction and I'll take this one. Right three steps forward in the direction you have been told to take and fire, then another three steps and fire, then you walk back to where you started but without taking your eyes off the direction you fired, do you understand?*'

There was silence.

'*Tell me you understand gentleman we haven't got time.*' shouted George.

'*Yes, yes, gotcha, yes sir, yes.*' The response's came.

'On my marks – *now* – one, two, three – *fire.*' The sounds of simultaneous gunshot scattered the silence, the echo sent birds flying and screaming.

'*One, two, three, - fire.*' The shots again cracked through the jungle like a whip snapping home. 'Now walk backwards slowly to where you started.' George commanded.

The men slowly marched backwards in unison to their original position with rifles poised, scanning their section of the Jungle with wide, fear filled eyes.

George without even thinking carried on giving orders, 'Inda, Vijay and myself will use the machete's to make this clearing bigger the rest of you have your guns primed and aimed and I mean aimed at the jungle, not at your side, not pointing at the ground.'

Vijay threw George a machete and as he caught it he turned and swung hard, violently taking out a large swathe of foliage as he did so.

Inda and Vijay immediately started hacking away at the jungle in all directions pushing the small space they had into a larger clearing.

'Sir come and look at this, quickly.' shouted Vijay.

George looked up and walked over to Vijay, the rest began to do the same.

'*Stay where you are – guns*, you bloody fools, keep them on the jungle.' Gerald went to say something but with George's vast experience in warfare he decided not to argue.

Alistair pointed back at the jungle with sweat dripping down his brow out of fright as much as from the heat.

'Look sir, look at the tree, look at the marks.'

George stepped over the bloody corpse and examined the tree.

'By Jove you are right Vijay.'

Vijay looked at Inda and Vijay who were craning their necks to have a look, his brown eyes looked full of wonder but not of some great marvel that fills you with joy but that of a terrifying mystery. 'That is no cat.' he said solemnly.

'What the hell are you talking about man? Make sense damn it.' snapped Alistair.

'Come on George you're vexing us, fess up.' said Gerald staring his friend dead in the eye.

'It hid in the tree.' replied George.

'It hid in the tree, it's a cat - of course it hid in the bloody tree.'

'No Gerald, you misunderstand, it hid in the tree and waited for us to walk by, this spot was the perfect place, one quick swipe with a claw and you have yourself a silent kill.'

'Are you telling me that a tiger intentionally ambushed us George?'

'That is exactly what I am telling you Gerald. Let's get back to work we need to keep on, we will discuss this after.'

The men worked feverishly under armed guard for half an hour cutting a large swathe out until the clearing was big enough for them to gather in safety. They sat on the floor with guns pointing in every direction.

'George, I think you overestimate this animal, it could not be smart enough to lure us down a single file track and then rip out one of our throats as we go by.' said Alistair.

'What if Charles was lured?' said Vijay, quietly coughing down in his hand wondering to himself whether he had spoken out of turn.

'Exactly.' said George nodding at Vijay.

'That's why I could not track it earlier, it had taken to the trees.' said Inda taking a large gulp of whisky and passing it around. The bottle circulated several times and the men soon discovered their anger, fear, despair and determination.

'Look Charles, by the intelligence that was gathered was thrown into the river and then killed by both crocodile and tiger. I didn't want to tell you this as I thought it would be too incredible to be of belief, but now you are seeing for yourselves, events unfolding that are ... well for want of a better word, unnatural. Charles was set up. The rope bridge had clear tiger prints running across it and then while he was halfway across the ropes were cut.' said George swigging heavily again from the bottle.

'Who did that to our friend?' cried Gerald, leaning forward and snatching the bottle from George's hand.

'That's just it; it was a tiger's claw that cut the ropes.' continued George.

'You bloody jest!' cried Alistair.

Inda looked at George knowingly and then back to Alistair. 'I am afraid he doesn't.'

'Stop hogging Gerald.' snapped Alistair snatching the half empty whisky bottle.

'It is as I said from the start, something is not right and tragedy has called upon us once again, we must pull back to the hotel.' said George

'All we have to do is outsmart it.'

'Stop being a bloody idiot Gerald, don't you get it, are you really too obtuse to see you are the one being hunted.' George lowered his voice. 'You think this is an accident that it came *closer* to camp, what you think it got lost? Tell me Gerald what would you do if you were laying somewhere with your wife when for no reason someone came along and shot her dead, what would you do eh? *What would you do?'*

'Stop being so melodramatic, it is completely different it is just an animal.' replied Gerald.

'So how has it been able to outsmart us all of the way, there was even tracks on both sides of the bank where it had swam back across, there is no other explanation with Charles, you show me an animal that can think and plan like that.'

'George it is just too incredulous I tell you.' shouted Alistair with a wildness coming to his eyes for the first time.

'Oh so sheer ignorance it is then.' retorted George.

'Look, I agree with you George but I will avenge my master and right my family's honour.' said Inda.

'It is just a cat and that is all it is if you ask me.' said Vijay.

'Well I warned you all, I shall return to the hotel immediately, you have a perimeter set up, I suggest you maintain it for a while, if you decide to camp make a large fire.'

As George said it, a solitary shot rang out through the jungle.

'That was a handgun.' said Inda.

George with impressive speed drew his revolver and fired it into the air.

'It is just the others trying to locate us.'

They all sat there waiting in silence, there was another shot but closer. George again returned fire, a few minutes later they heard voices and branches being chopped and trodden on.'

It was then that the men appeared, all five of them.

'Thank God you are all safe.' said Vijay. 'I am afraid we have not been so lucky, he said pointing towards the body, the men looked aghast and frightened.'

Two of the men looked at each other with terror in their eyes, they turned to run.

'Where do you think you're going?' said Vijay firing his pistol.

The men turned back. 'Sorry but we believe this tiger is not of earth it is surely a ghost.'

Gerald slapped his forehead. He stood up. '*Look this tiger has killed our friends are we going to kill that bloody cat or what.*' He started pacing the perimeter. '*I am not afraid, I have no fear, I am not afraid of you.*'

'*You are right Gerald.*' shouted Inda rising to his feet.

'*Yes, let's get us a trophy.*' cried Alistair in a drunken roar.

George watched in despair as his friends danced around like idiots drinking, shouting and claiming invincibility, he knew what he had witnessed, he knew this cat had set about avenging those who had killed its kin. The whisky and extra manpower had reduced their intellects whilst exaggerating their courage, they passed the whisky around more and more, by now George who was himself a little inebriated had stopped consuming it for his own safety.

He could not help but wonder whether he would ever see his friends again. He knew they would never be swayed by rationality. Giving no thought to his own perilous journey he waited patiently for them to settle down.

'I'm sorry, but I must go.' he said putting his light beige canvas backpack on. George walked forward to Gerald, whose slick hair shone like frost on black ice.

'Please come with me my friend,' said George grabbing Gerald's arm firmly, 'have you ever known me to act like this before?'

'No, you know I haven't, but please, I implore you George, stay, join the hunt, we can get this creature, especially with your help.'

'You know I cannot stay but promise me, promise me my friend, that you will at least sober up first, I tell you the drink has hold of you - and you Alistair.' George said turning to Alistair.

'George we shall be fine, we may have crossed words but I really do not wish us to part ways at this juncture, we are all good friends. Are we not united by the death of our friend Charles? Let us just see it out together and then we can put it behind us, within twenty four hours we shall be stuffing our faces and laughing about all this.'

'Or we will be sitting around without our throats torn out. Look we are both irremovable on this, I am sticking to my word and trekking back to the vehicles or the hotel, whichever one I find first.'

'On your own? You must be bloody mad.' said Gerald.

'You know what, *you need a bloody drink*.' said Alistair thrusting a bottle into George's hands. George knocked back several large gulps, his eyes misting over a crimson colour as he did so.

'My friends I confront my fate like a man, I shall trek through the Jungle loudly, if the tiger chooses to confront me then we will fight valiantly.' George said handing the bottle to Gerald.

'*Then at least take them two bloody cowards with you.*' said Alistair. The two men who had tried to run away earlier looked shamefully at the ground. Gerald grabbed Alistair's arm. 'That's enough.' Gerald said looking Alistair in the eye.

Inda walked over. 'Sir I concur, at the very least you should take some men with you.'

'*Confound you all*, I am going alone, I do not fear.' said George looking at Vijay.

'I know you don't Sir.' said Vijay wondering how he had read his mind earlier.

'Now I must go, God speed and good luck, I truly pray that I will see you all safe and well again soon.'

George walked off across the clearing and disappeared into the thick Jungle without looking back.

Gerald and Alistair stood there watching him disappear.

'Sir, the men would like to bury the body and say goodbye.'

Gerald snapped out of his stupor. 'That is fine Vijay can you get it all done in an hour.'

'Should be able to.'

'Good then go ahead and Vijay you may address me as Gerald.'

'Very good Gerald, thank you.'

The five men and Vijay dug a grave within fifteen minutes then spent the next forty five minutes offering prayers, Inda joined in at that point.

Gerald and Alistair took the opportunity to eat and talk, then they drank some more, the men returned after an hour and thanked Gerald for allowing them to bury their comrade. Gerald then instructed that they eat after they all had a drink in memoriam to those who had died. A bottle of whisky was passed around until it was emptied.

'We must be getting on, for it is nearly afternoon.' said Inda.

The men by now were all sitting comfortably.

'Well Inda what is the plan?' asked Alistair mopping his brow with a sweat sodden handkerchief.

'I guess we have no choice but to track, don't you think?'

'We could just stay here for a while.' said Gerald laying back.

The sun blazed, the whisky became three times as strong. Gerald swatted his neck with a loud stinging slap. 'Bloody Mosqweetoes.' he said.

'*Mosqweeetoes*, old boy.' said Alistair laughing heartily, 'perhaps you ought to slow down.'

'Perhaps we should go and kill ourselves a tiger.' said Gerald jumping up.

'I was afraid of this, the drink has got to you.' Alistair said despairing at the heat.

'Then have a drink.' said Gerald throwing him a bottle.

Alistair caught it and had a drink. 'It is just too hot to do anything.' Alistair turned and saw Vijay and the five remaining men chatting genially.

Inda was watching him and laughed. 'We are used to it, it is merely warm today.'

'Warm? Confound you, it's like a furnace.' he said mopping his brow and swiping a large insect off his trousers. 'And these bloody bugs are driving me crazy.'

'Come on let us get on with the hunt.' said Gerald who was still standing, scanning the periphery with his rifle aimed.

'Let us have some water.' said Alistair pulling out a large canteen. He unscrewed the top and drunk heavily. He passed the canteen to Gerald.

'Very well then.' he said gulping it back himself, as he drunk he looked again at the five remaining hunters and noticed that they had all stopped drinking and were now consuming a lot of water.

Vijay turned his head and realised what they were looking at. 'You must drink water to keep hydrated and alert, it is not just tigers you have to worry about in the jungle.' he said softly.

Gerald returned the canteen and Alistair looked at him briefly before committing to another series of large gulps.

'Well it is a bloody tiger that concerns me at the moment.' said Alistair.

'Nonsense Alistair, look how many of us there are.' said Gerald gesturing to all the men with his hand.

'But it still managed to get one of us didn't it?' responded Alistair.

'How do we know it was even the same bloody cat, it could have been any, perhaps it was asleep in a tree we passed and woke it, it panicked, attacked and fled.'

'Oh shut up Gerald, it is the same tiger and *you* know it is.' retorted Alistair rather hotly. Suddenly there was an outburst from one of the *shikari's* who said something in Hindi.

'What is he rabbiting about Vijay?' said Gerald impatiently.

Vijay turned to answer, 'he said ...' the canteen stopped halfway to his mouth, which had dropped agape as if his jaw muscles had suddenly vanished.

'What on earth is wrong with you all, answer the damned question.' said Gerald looking at Vijay and the shikari's who all looked visibly shaken, some of them even appeared to be praying.

'He said ... it is the same tiger.' said Inda looking to Gerald. *'Sir Look!'* Inda shouted.

'Good God!' shouted Alistair in shock. The whole party stared, for on the edge of the clearing about twenty metres away was the tiger. It was sitting there with a blood soaked mouth watching them.

'It's leg, the scar. It is the same one.' said Inda pointing desperately.

The tiger turned and jumped back into the thick undergrowth as Gerald's rifle spoke. Without warning Gerald sprinted to toward the jungle after the giant cat. Inda leapt up, and motioned for Vijay who also jumped to his feet, as he did all the other men got up, they all ran toward the jungle. Alistair rifled up and ran with them.

The party trying to catch up with Gerald heard a shot just up ahead of them, they kept on forward, they heard another two shots. Alistair found his courage and pushed himself to the front.

'Missed the blasted thing, three shots I had and I still missed.' said Gerald stepping out of some thick leaves.

'Don't do that you bloody idiot, I nearly shot you.' said Alistair.

'Sorry chap did I startle you.' Gerald replied smiling.

'Not funny.' said Alistair.

The leaves were thick and intrusive, the party had stopped uncomfortably amongst them.

'Inda, can you track it?' asked Gerald.

'Yes, should be easy but I suggest we go back, we have left our bags and supplies behind, to carry on would be fool hardy.'

'He is right Gerald.' said Alistair, his large frame looking at odds with the surroundings.

'I know, well let's be quick about it.' Gerald replied pushing his way back toward the camp. Alistair followed and everyone fell in line behind them.

'Do not distress, this has galvanised me into action, let's stick together and run it down.'

'Now you're talking Alistair, that's what I like to hear.' said Gerald turning to his colleague with a beaming smile across his face.

Upon collecting their bags they did a quick inventory check, after checking their guns were ready to fire and that the ammo was easily reached, they retraced their steps back into the jungle.

The heat was stifling, oxygen seemed to be robbed from them before the air could hit their lungs, their skin was rapidly turning red from repeated slapping and scratching as every exposed part crawled with insects and flies.

The party followed Inda's lead as he confidently tracked, there was not much talk, they were all on what they perceived to be their highest alert for the alcohol had taken its toll. The Shikari's had drunk the least and were relatively unscathed, Inda had drunk enough to affect him, so had Vijay but Gerald and Alistair albeit fairly compos mentis were affected, little did Gerald realise that if it were not for the alcohol he would have made that third shot.

'He isn't far.' said Inda hacking some leaves out of the way with his machete. There was a loud roar.

'It came from over there.' shouted Alistair.

The party changed direction slightly and within a minute or two came across a well-worn track.

'The cheeky devil is using the path.' said Gerald.

'They often do.' added Inda.

They walked along the path, the men were able to congregate a little better and they moved as a tight group, until they came upon a fork in the road.

'What do you think?' said Gerald to Inda who was on the ground trying to pick up the track.

'This ground is nothing but bone dry mud, and too wide, he can move without trace.'

'The men say it is because it is a ghost – an avenging spirit.' said Vijay.

'What a load of bloody twoddle.' said Gerald scratching the back of his leg with his other foot.

'Our people believe in such things.' said Inda looking up.

'Well whatever it is, it looks like we are going to have to guess the direction it took, if we want to find it.' Gerald replied as if he had not heard Inda's previous point.

'Come on Inda you're supposed to be one of the best trackers around.' said Alistair swatting a fly on his neck.

'That maybe but not even the best tracker in the world can find tracks that aren't there.' said Inda slowly standing up.

'He has a point.' Gerald said rubbing his chin.

Just then another roar rang through the jungle, it was clearly coming from the left hand path. The men immediately set off down it.

'This is the day sir I know it is.' said Vijay.

'Yes I'll agree with that.' said Alistair.

'Then it is a deal, we run the cat down and argue over a bottle of whisky who will keep the hide.' Gerald said lifting his rifle as he said it.

'I'll drink to that.' said Alistair. A small laugh broke out.

'So will I.' said Inda.

There was another roar up ahead.

'Come on.' said Vijay 'We're closing in.' He and some others ran to the front, the whole group broke into a jog. They heard some deer barking.

The hunting party came out into a wide elongated clearing which was clearly used as a trail of sorts, they looked ahead and saw the tiger sitting in the middle of the track swishing its tail just where the track began to round a corner.

The men raised their rifles. Thousands of bats fled from their leafy rooftops as a cacophony of shots shattered the Jungle tranquillity. The tiger disappeared around the corner with bullets dancing after it.

'Come on, we have the bugger on the run, *chase it down.*' said Gerald dropping his pack and running forward as fast as he could, Vijay and Alistair did also, but one of the Shikari's was already after it, he and Gerald were formidably fast runners.

They ran ahead but Inda had stopped in his tracks. A strange and terrible feeling overcome him, a malevolent phantom robbed him of action as he tried to place the feeling, something familiar, something not as it should be, he looked and saw Gerald and the Shikari racing for the corner to get a shot at the fleeing beast, the rest of the party hastened after them – a thought – an image – more than that, *de ja vu*, no, it was a memory.

Horror filled Inda's eyes *'Wait, stop, stop, Gerald, stop now, stop right now.'* But his words were too late he watched as Gerald and the Shikari disappeared from view.

Inda sprinted toward them. The others all stopped in their tracks. It took a minute or two for Inda to catch up and realise his worst fear, this tiger, this king of beasts had led them once again into a horrifying trap but this time it was a trap set by man himself.

Down below them, Gerald and the *shikari* had fallen into the trap dug by the men, they laid there impaled upon sharpened sticks and large spears, which had skewered through them. Gerald's foot twitched slightly in the last throes of death as a large sharpened spear sat bludgeoned through his midriff, blood and insides hung off the end as if purposefully decorated.

The shikari had a large stick through his leg, one through his shoulder but worse than that, one had smashed its way through his skull and out of his eye.

There was a loud wailing as the two men who had earlier ran lost their minds to fear, they started chanting and shouting all manner of words.

'They are saying that the tiger is the avenging spirit sent to destroy those who are evil and without virtue.' said Vijay.

'You bloody what?' said Alistair looking up with tear filled eyes.

'They say that when we killed the tigress we destroyed an innocent love, now we are to be destroyed.'

'What a load of bollocks – it can't …'

There were a couple of cries, the two men ran into the jungle petrified. Vijay immediately drew his gun and went to go after them but Alistair stopped him, 'leave them Inda, we don't want cowards. They will probably come running back once they realise that they're on their own.'

Alistair, Inda, Vijay and the two remaining shikari's all stood in a line staring in disbelief at their friend's speared corpses.

Alistair fell to one knee. 'Oh Gerald,' he gasped as he wept bitterly into his hand, after a brief moment he stood up again, 'how do we get this bloody thing?' he said re-cocking his gun.

'The bodies sir, we must bury them as we have no time for cremation.' said Vijay.

'Not this time, we have to get this beast and now.'

'Or we could retreat sir.' said Vijay running his hand through his black hair rather nervously.

'Don't you get it we are the ones being hunted, we are all going to die, we are the only ones endangered around here and now my friend …' Alistair choked for a second fighting back tears. *'And now my friend is dead.'*

'I fear you are right Alistair, I have never known anything like it.' said Inda kicking the ground in frustration as the diminished platoon of assisting shikari's and trackers chanted and prayed in the background.

Vijay looked at Alistair and Inda in a moment of pure sincerity as they stood staring at the mangled corpses. Alistair and Inda could feel Vijay's desire to talk, they tore themselves away from their torturous transfixion and looked up at him.

'I must say to you both, I am afraid. I have hunted and killed many, many things but only now do I know what it is like to be hunted, maybe *we* are the monsters.'

'Vijay keep it together there's a good chap, look, we are all afraid, I am still not sure exactly what is happening but let us not forget it has a scar down its leg and I have yet to meet a ghost that has cut itself.'

They all gave a small albeit nervous laugh.

'Now somebody give me a bloody drink.' said Alistair. Inda threw the bottle he had picked up off the ground when they had left the clearing. He guzzled from it heavily and after pouring some into the pit reluctantly started to walk away.

They heard a roar, accompanied by several gun shots and a scream coming from deep in the jungle. The men all ran into foliage, smashing their way through with energy and determination, overriding the fear that was slowly growing inside each one of them. It took a good few minutes until they came across the first body. His face and throat was an undecipherable mess, they followed the trail of blood that had been dripping from the tiger's mouth to the second corpse. He was laying on his front, huge claws had torn up his back like a ploughed field, his neck had been bitten out from the back leaving his spinal cord exposed with a fairly large kink where the tiger had literally started pulling it out of him.

'Confound this murderous beast. Come on, back the way we came, quick.' said Alistair.

Vijay turned and motioned to the two who were at the back, they instantly turned around and took the lead heading the party back to where they had come from.

They emerged into the scorching heat, by now they all looked dishevelled, Alistair's curly hair had debris from trees and plants in almost every curl.

'Inda we must have a plan.' said Vijay.

'I agree, let us get ourselves together and try to outthink this thing.' said Inda.

'Why don't we all congregate somewhere but have one man sneak through the jungle and creep up behind it.' said Alistair, fumbling in his pocket for extra ammo.

'That will not work, the inevitable will happen.' said Inda looking away deep in thought.

'Yes you are right old chap, a foolish plan.' said Alistair. 'It must be this blasted heat going to my head.'

One of the two remaining Shikari's stepped forward and in broken English said. 'Whatever we do, we need do it fast it getting dark soon.'

'He is right, what will we do at night, not even a fire will keep this tiger at bay.' said Vijay.

'No, he'll probably barbecue *us* on it.' said Alistair laughing heartily at his own joke, Vijay joined in but Inda just paid it lip service.

'*Water!* Maybe if we can find water we could have a chance.'

'What on earth do you mean old boy?' said Alistair.

'Let us carry on walking, we use this clearing, but keep vigilant.' said Inda still reflecting on his plan.

'Of course I am going to keep vigilant, what a bloody stupid thing to say, now come on, out with your plan, you are not on her majesty's secret service.' said Alistair with flushed cheeks.

'I was thinking if we could find a riverbank, especially one with a large exposed shore, the tiger would be forced to come into the open to get us. We could light a fire at night so we can see it coming and with the water on the other side it would not be able to come ashore without attracting attention.'

'What about crocodiles?' asked Vijay.

'*This* tiger might not be afraid of what burns it, but crocodiles certainly are, in fact that is just as much a reason for the fire.' replied Inda.

'And psychological welfare.' said Alistair.

Inda gave him a strange look but said nothing.

'It sounds like a plan.' said Vijay turning and translating it to the two other men who nodded their agreement.

'We still have to find a river ... but other than that.' Alistair said wiping the sweat from the back of his neck with a handkerchief.

'Leave that to me.' said Inda confidently looking up out of his thought filled trance.

With guns cocked they walked along the widened clearing as it snaked its way through the jungle like a river of grass. After ten minutes of walking in silence they were greeted by a cul-de-sac.

'It just ends in dense Jungle, how are we supposed to last in there?' said Alistair.

'What choice do we have?' replied Inda solemnly.

Vijay gulped as the men once again entered the jungle.

'Something is not right it is quiet, I mean too quiet, I hear no monkeys, no birds, not even any insects.' said Alistair.

'It is eerie.' said Inda.

They crept forward trying not to make noise but failing with every step, yet every time they stopped there was no sound.

'That tiger has been tracking us the whole way, I know it has. This is a bad omen, I feel it.'

'Vijay, you are being frightfully unhelpful to the situation.' said Alistair throwing him a stare.

'Sorry, it's just that it could jump out at any minute. In fact I am expecting it to.'

'Well you are an idiot then.' retorted Alistair hotly.

A twig snapped some distance away, they all spun round with their guns trained in the direction of the sound, unwelcome sweat pulsated out of their foreheads as fear mixed with the stifling heat, yet not one man would dare let a hand leave his weapon to wipe it away no matter how much it tickled, aggravated and tortured them.

'There isn't a sound, is it stalking us?' asked Alistair.

'I don't know, but I would have to say probably.' replied Inda.

'The men all looked at each other.'

'We should keep moving.' said Inda treading lightly forward, the men continued sweeping, the barrels of their guns moving in unison with their heads in all directions. Yet there was still nothing.

'Why do I feel that we are being toyed with?' said Alistair.

'Because we are.' said Vijay quietly.

One of the men came from behind and said something to Vijay.

'The men say that there is no escaping, they are terrified that we cannot appease this angry spirit, the feline avenger will claim us all and devour our souls.' said Vijay translating for Alistair.

They trudged on in the eerie quiet, the darkness stalked, enveloping them until they were wandering blind through the land of snakes and shadows.

Individually they all started offering their prayers. Alistair in his mind, but the others with one of their hands, taking it off the gun for just the briefest of seconds, he said nothing but when Alistair saw that even Inda was praying his heart beat increased, he felt panic fighting for control of his body.

'Any sign of this confounded river yet?' asked Alistair.

'No, said Inda 'it is hard to see in this dark, in the moments when the moonlight breaks through I get a glimpse.'

'What are you looking for?' asked Alistair.

'Any sign that we are near water.' responded Inda keeping his eyes in the foliage.

'I thought it was supposed to be cold at night in the desert.' Alistair said wiping his neck with his sweat sodden handkerchief which by now only added sweat, making the matter worse.

'We are not in the desert we are in the jungle.' said Vijay.

'But I feel even hotter than I did earlier, I'm chaffing all over.' Alistair replied almost whining.

'It is the humidity you feel.' said Inda.

'The men continued, sweat poured from every orifice, sores and rashes broke out where ever the skin met. Equipment and supplies grew ever more heavy and burdensome. They walked without incident, yet the tiger haunted and possessed their every step, the footmen had terrible daydreams of the ghost cat coming for them. Behind every leaf brushed aside the hunters expected to be greeted by the orange eyes of death, every twig that snapped they feared the tiger's claw, every movement in the trees the shikari's saw giant fangs snap at them, they began to shake out of fear and exhaustion, the alcohol wore off, the bravery subsided and hope began to fade as they hacked their way through the jungle with the desperation of a caged animal gnawing at metal bars for its freedom.'

'Where is this tiger? We haven't heard anything for hours, maybe it has had enough and left.' said Alistair in a meek tone as if fearing the answer.

'It could be three feet away and you wouldn't know, it is playing with us, does anyone else think it has left?' asked Inda stopping and looking around momentarily. He was greeted by a wall of silence 'No I thought not.' He looked around, as he was about to carry on walking ...

'But look what I have found; this is what I have been looking for.' Inda said excitedly grabbing a plant. 'We are near water.'

'Thank God for that.' exclaimed Alistair. 'How do you know?'

'Because these plants only grow near water.'

'But what way is it?'

'I am not sure, there seem to be more in that direction.'

The party changed direction and followed the flowers that were barely distinguishable in the moonlight, as they walked the Jungle thinned out.

'Stop!' said Inda in a loud voice. 'Look.' He said pointing ahead.

'By Jove we nearly walked straight into the river.' said Alistair stopping in his tracks, suddenly realising that he was right on the bank of a large river.

'We need to move along the edge quickly to try and find a suitable spot.' said Alistair.

'Yes, let's follow the direction of the river.' said Vijay.

'What does it matter what way we go?' enquired Alistair.

'The current will sweep round corners.'

'Excellent point Vijay.' said Inda finally rubbing his own neck and face. 'As the river sweeps round corners it deposits large amounts of silt creating the sort of beaches and mud banks we are looking for.'

'Inda you might as well carry on taking point as soon as you know what we are looking for.' said Alistair with a slight authority returning to his voice.

They marched with a moderately stronger step. Albeit they were actually in more danger than before the men felt safer as if the river might protect them, even though crocodiles and snakes often lurked in its murky waters.

They walked for about fifteen minutes when the river widened out into a moonlit bay. A wide beach swept around a bend creating a large gap between the water and dense jungle. Best of all there was a large, wide strip of long grass between the beach and jungle, several large rocks were also dotted around with a couple of stand-alone trees.

'That looks bloody perfect, I couldn't have designed it better myself.' said Alistair.

'Quick, get in the open.' The men all ran for the clearing as they remembered the danger they were in, forgetting themselves they hugged each other jubilantly upon arrival.

The moon canvassed the whole area silver. It was difficult to distinguish where the river stopped and the sand started. Standing there surveying the scene the men glanced upon each other and were surprised to see the state they were all in, their trek through the jungle had taken a visible toll.

Inda instructed everyone to take food and water while they had the chance, they all congregated around a large rock.

Inda sat on it with his rifle not taking his eye off the jungle even whilst eating, drinking and rifling through his bag. The others naturally arranged themselves in defensive positions, each man keeping an eye on a different direction, even the water was covered such was their paranoia.

'It is so good to sit down.' said Vijay.

'Tell me about it, my legs feel like cricket stumps – they've been knocked for six.' said Alistair.

The men had a small laugh at this but it was a fleeting moment and as Inda surveyed the horizon, he began to formulate their best course of action.

Experience and skill alone made Inda the clear leader albeit Alistair just by his social and aristocratic status was supposedly so. Alistair had already realised Inda was the natural leader, although he knew it to be true and prudence would even lend itself to the fact, he still found himself subconsciously fighting it.

'Inda come up with a plan for us, there's a good chap.' he said.

Inda looked down at his interlocutor and then back at the Jungle.

'I took the liberty of starting already.' he said. 'Some of these rocks give us a good vantage point and one of those trees should give us a clear shot from the side if we use it as a makeshift machan. Then use the rock over there to cover the person in the tree. Yes I believe we have the perfect scenario, there is no way he can get in and out without one of us having a clear shot.'

'It is not that clear, the grass at the back is long enough especially as it is dark and even more especially as that is exactly why the bloody thing has stripes.' said Alistair swigging some water back.

'You are correct Alistair, but you miss the point, that is why it is perfect there is no point in having a place where it has no chance to hide or stalk, it simply wouldn't come. The tiger has already proved it is not stupid, but we know there is only one place it can come from. We just have to remain vigilant and I do mean vigilant. There is not enough of us to be anything less than scrupulous, we have just enough men, each one of us will be as vital as the other.' replied Inda. 'Who is the best shot here?'

'You are Inda, this is not the best time to be fishing for blasted compliments.' said Alistair staring at him incredulously.

'In situations like this, one does not assume or boast. So the question becomes where should the best shot be placed?'

'Up the tree.' said Vijay.

'We need a good shot up there, but I am not sure that would be the *hardest* shot to take.' Alistair said.

Inda rubbed his chin. 'I am thinking the ground level shot will be the hardest, Vijay you are a very good shot. From the vantage point in the tree and in the clear moonlight you should easily be able to make it.'

'I am not good at climbing though.' said Vijay.

'We can all help with that.' said Alistair.

'Again if the tiger goes for you in the tree Vijay and one of your men take point behind that rock and train his rifle at the bottom of the tree it should be an easy, clear shot. Then if Alistair and Arshad sit around the fire, not too near, but close enough to be of temptation, then I can get on that large jagged rock behind you as that will require the best shot.'

'Inda, perhaps I should stand behind the rock and you sit by the fire.' said Alistair.

'With the greatest of respect sir, if you are sure that you will have the best chance of hitting and stopping a fully grown male tiger charging at full speed out of nowhere then

I shall gladly swap.' Inda replied looking at Alistair earnestly.

'Confound you Inda, I suppose you are correct, but it'd better be a bloody big fire.'

'Yes, I know what to look for in the jungle and we will not have to go far in. Vijay have your men collect some wood, tell them we will all go together, with us three behind them with guns drawn the whole time.'

Vijay relayed the message and the men once again went into the Jungle, they had almost forgotten the danger they were in as they made their plans, but now once again trepidation pounced upon them with vengeance.

They held their breath as the men lifted the vegetation searching for dry wood, they were native to the jungle and knew its secrets, not long after with big armfuls of wood, the party headed back to the beach. They even walked backwards with their barrels trained on the jungle expecting a surprise attack as they came out.

'You know in a weird way I wish the bloody thing would make an appearance, I can't stand this, it is too quiet, I tell you if I never hunt again I care not and any man who has something to say about that, I shall show him Queensbury rules if he does by Jove.' said Alistair.

'The men still say that we are foolish to do anything but pray.' said Vijay.

'Perhaps they are right.' said Alistair sighing deeply.

'This has to work, it cannot come out of the water without attracting attention, and if it tries to come from the side it has to cross open beach, no it is only the front that offers an opportunity and that is exactly where we want it to come from. We will end this now. Vijay prepare yourself, we will all escort you, the two men will help you, myself and Alistair will cover you with rifles.' said Inda.

Vijay and the two men headed across the beach and into the waist high long grass, on tenterhooks Alistair and Inda stalked forward with rifles cocked and drawn, they walked slowly with their barrels facing forward. Listening intently, they knew that this was the most dangerous moment that they faced, they were in the long grass, a tiger's speciality.

Again nothing but stillness and their own heartbeats, no twig snapping, no birds flapping, no leaves rustling. They reached the tree, Inda and Alistair stood cautiously back.

The men helped Vijay get up the tree but once he was up onto the first major branch he ably climbed to a good vantage point. He managed to find a series of long thick branches to lie on, they enabled him to train his rifle comfortably and steadily on the small meadow of long grass.

'I suddenly feel jealous.' Inda said.

'He does look comfortable doesn't he?' Alistair said stepping backwards as the men came towards them.

They allowed the men to catch up, then retreated back onto the beach. Looking up they could see the outline of Vijay laying in the tree, from afar he looked like a plastic toy soldier.

'What are their names?' enquired Alistair pointing at the two remaining shikari's.

'The one with the moustache is Arshad and the one with the scar on his cheek is Eckachandra.'

Alistair, Eckachandra and Arshad officially acknowledged each other with a shallow nod.

Inda spoke to Eckachandra in Hindi, he nodded and took up position behind a rock with his rifle aimed squarely at the base of the tree in which Vijay was positioned.

Inda then built a capable fire about fifteen metres in from the grass line, the flames leapt high, Alistair couldn't help but smile.

Alistair and Arshad sat down around the fire, they both pulled out their revolvers and after double checking the load, cocked them both.

'You're sure you can hit this thing Inda?' said Alistair the dirt on his face flickering like war paint in the light of the fire.

'I can, but this tiger is no ordinary cat, I would advise you to keep alert with guns at the ready.' Inda repeated it to Arshad who after nodding his acknowledgement turned and nodded to Alistair.

Inda silently retreated. He went to the large rock which had two ledges one about waist height and the other about six feet higher. He climbed on to the lower shelf. Once his gun was trained he raised his hand. Eckachandra who was covering Vijay across the beach raised his hand in response, Alistair and Arshad raised theirs as well.

Alistair watched the tree intently and in the moonlight could just make out a shadow waving, he then looked back at Inda and gave a thumbs up. The game had begun.

They waited, all the men stationed away from the fire found themselves taunted by it burning in the distance, it looked so safe and welcoming, as if it could heal all their worries and solve their calamity. The men fought to cling on to their concentration, not forgetting that the man next to them had placed his life in their hands.

The minutes passed but the jungle provided no comfort, no sounds of life, no sign of dawn, they were lost and desperate with one plan, just one hope of coming out of this with their lives. Each man reflected on their actions, what could they have done to bring such wrath upon them, where was this karma from, what God persecuted them so, had they really destroyed something divine when the tigress was slain? Maybe it was just blood thirsty revenge on those who had killed the one it loved.

Isolated - nothing but their fear, paranoia and ruminations to keep them company. As the minutes threatened to turn into hours their eyes began to grow heavy, they were fatigued, exhausted, mentally drained, could a moment's sleep really do any harm? Perhaps the tiger wouldn't come, perhaps it had sated it's hatred for man.

Vijay shook his head violently to keep himself awake.

Alistair's head dropped, he quickly snapped his head back up only to have it start lowering again after a few seconds. Arshad did not seem to notice as he scanned the grass line that the lines were becoming blurred, crisscrossed as lethargy surreptitiously crept in.

But Eckanchandra covering the base of the tree had given into his silent tormentor, his head lay on the butt of his rifle. Vijay fought to stay alert, oblivious that no one was watching his back.

An hour passed, Inda felt his eyes rolling but knew he could not allow himself to fall asleep. His eyes swept lazily across the horizon as his head finally went down, 'I must sleep, I can't …' he said to himself. As he did a tiny pulse ebbed through him, another thought, what had he just seen ... a movement ... a flicker ... a flicker of the fire ... no it wasn't, *it was in the grass!*

Inda jolted awake, his eyes had grasped one last look at the horizon as he was succumbing to slumber. He had definitely seen a flicker in the grass as if something was moving through it, his heartbeat kicked into gear and adrenaline surged through his body like a herd of stampeding antelopes.

He scanned the meadow and saw the grass tops move ever so slightly at odds with the environment. Inda was praying that Vijay had seen it, he looked to the side and to his horror realised that the man watching Vijay had fallen asleep. Inda looked back at the fire and saw that neither Alistair nor Arshad was in a position to get a shot off in time.

Inda's heart raced, the grass moved again, if he tried to alert anyone he might scare it off. At last they had the upper hand. They could end this thing once and for all. He tried to guess it's direction, if it was going for Vijay he would have no choice but to take a shot just to wake everyone up.

The grass moved again it was coming for the fire, he aimed at the top of the stalks that were moving but he had no shot. It was still a long way off but now wide awake Inda tracked it as it skulked forward.

Without warning his rifle flew out of his hands, he just managed to catch it before it fell off the rock, Alistair and Arshad bolted upright, Eckachandra leapt up in a panic, realising that he had fallen asleep – a shot had rang out through the still night, their hearts jumped as another one rang out.

'Yes, yes I got him, I got him, the tiger is dead, it's dead.' shouted Vijay as loudly as he could, climbing down from the tree, the moon was shining bright still, they could see his silhouette quite clearly as he made his way through the grass toward them and the dead tiger.

'Everyone else stay where you are.' shouted Inda as Alistair got up and went to walk forward. Alistair stopped, they all watched Vijay walking through the meadow.

Vijay reached the cats body.

'Don't forget to check for the scar.' shouted Alistair.

Vijay looked down and there laying in the grass was a large big cat, he prodded it with his rifle, it did not move, he hit it again but harder, but there was still no movement, he ventured in for a closer inspection.

The only thing on his mind was checking for the scar on its leg, it was then that he realised something. They were not stripes on the cat's body, they were patches – this wasn't a tiger!

'It's a Leopard.' shouted Vijay.

'What, we can't hear you.' shouted Alistair. Inda finally left his post, with his rifle in hand he ran to the fire.

'It's a Jeopard?.' replied Inda shouting. 'What is he shouting Alistair?'

'I don't know Inda something about a leopard I think.'

'A leopard, what about a leopard? ... No wait, no *Vijjjaaayyyyyy*!' screamed Inda, his heart raced as he looked up and watched the moonlight come alive and transform into a huge black and silver striped phantom cat. It leapt through the air and jet black oil was spurted asunder as Vijay was torn to pieces.

'*Vijayyyyyy.*' Inda screamed running into the long grass, Eckachandra abandoned his post by the rock and ran after him.

'I ... I cannot fight anymore, I sacrifice myself, I will let this angry God have it's revenge, at least I die with honour.' said Arshad, his smooth skin looking at odds against his black moustache.

'Don't talk so bloody stupid, hang on, I thought you could not speak English?'

'No sir, you assumed I could not, I speak it very well.'

'Well, what are you babbling on about then?'

'I know you do not understand,' Arshad replied throwing his rifle into the sand, then taking off his ammo belt and weapon holster and tossing them aside also.'

Alistair stood there watching him, scratching his head, filling with panic.

'Right, well you can do what you bloody well like but I still have the upper hand and if you want to be bait then that is your choice.' said Alistair turning and running to the large jagged rock that Inda had been using to cover them.

He climbed on the ledge and laid down training his rifle toward the fire just as Inda had. 'Bloody fool.' said Alistair nestling himself next to the wall of rock that went up to the higher ledge.

Albeit he was only waist height off the floor he felt he a good vantage point. Alistair realised he was breathing heavily, hyperventilating almost, his nerves rattling like guitar strings, fear was setting in and panic was becoming his master - he could fire a gun and hit a target but nowhere near the level of Inda and Charles.

He waited watching Arshad praying next to the fire with a profound curiosity. Something else also plagued his mind; where was Inda and Eckachandra, how were they faring, were they dead? He had heard no shots or screams, the jungle again - hauntingly silent.

It was still dark, there was no sign of dawn on the horizon, the lake of silver sand beamed moonlight, Alistair watched the grass studiously for any movement in the hope that he would get some warning before the need to take a shot.

He pondered whether he had made the right decision, he decided that he had, he was in a safe position with food and drink, and his back pack was next to him. There was also a high chance a boat would come by the next day, he could get safely back to civilization. The more he thought about it the more he hoped that the tiger would not come.

He also began to hope that Inda and Eckachandra would return whole and well. Alistair realised that his sacrificial friend was right, who cares who wins? He could be back at the hotel enjoying a meal with a few drinks and laughs. A large drop of water hit his hair rolled down one of his curls and dropped onto his face.

'Rain' - he hadn't thought of that. 'Please don't rain now.' he said to himself. Another drop splashed violently on his face but this time landing on his cheek. He quickly wiped it away replacing his hand on the gun as quickly as he could.

The adrenalin surged through him, his concentration was sharp, he was ever more confident of his position. 'Yes, when the men return we shall create a defensive perimeter around this rock with the sole aim of defence and await dawn. A fishing boat is bound to happen by.' he thought to himself.

Another large globule of water splashed down on his cheek,

'What is that blasted dripping?' he said to himself looking up. To his horror he saw the huge face of a snarling tiger and giant fangs coming towards him.

Alistair could feel warm liquid pouring down his neck and back, a faint sense of his limbs knocking on rock, then dragging on sand, an odd sensation, he breathed hot stale pungent breath which was not his own. Stars bounced past, he noticed how beautiful the moon was and then ... darkness.

The tiger dropped the lifeless body further up the beach, it looked at Arshad and then ran towards him.

~

The scream was heard deep in the jungle albeit faintly. Inda and Eckachandra stopped immediately.

'It must have double backed, we need to return to the camp.' said Inda.

Inda and Eckachandra had ran into the jungle after the tiger, not stopping even when moonlight ceased to penetrate the canopy. Inda's glowing anger shone the way, with adrenaline pumping they kept on believing they were closing in on their quarry but the cunning cat had turned back already.

'We cannot see though Inda.'

'Listen Eckachandra we have to get back, I am going to kill this cat if it is the last thing I do.' Inda said spluttering back tears.

'I know Inda but are you telling me you do not believe this to be an angry ghost or spirit sent by some deity?'

'This beast holy or not has killed too many of my friends, I must quench their thirst for vengeance and slay this clawed terror.'

'I pray that it would be so, but I fear it will not be.'

The men attempted to hack their way in the direction of the muffled scream but the going was tough. It was so dark that they could hardly see even after their eyes adjusted. Inda was experienced, he had been in the Jungle at night many times but it had never seemed this dark to him.

'It is impossible to see Inda, we have no choice, we must light a torch, the tiger probably will not even see it through this dense jungle.'

'This tiger has Mother India in its eyes, it can see everything.'

'That maybe, but *we* can't see *anything* Inda.'

'Come on we must press on, it will be on the move if we don't and I expect some sort of trap when we get to the beach.'

'Look Inda, look.' said Eckachandra, pointing through a small gap in the canopy. 'That is why we cannot see.'

'It has turned cloudy on us.' remarked Inda.

The men battled on through the thick foliage but progress was slow, the men had kept their packs on their back for precaution in case they should be the victim of a swipe from the back.

Inda lead, battling his way through the undergrowth with Eckachandra struggling behind, whenever they looked, the heavens were in turmoil with black clouds boiling across the sky.

After another twenty minutes they grew fatigued.

'Inda, how can you be sure that we are still heading the right way?' asked Eckachandra stopping and pulling an energy biscuit out of his pocket.

Inda looked into the blackness. 'I cannot be certain but let us keep moving.'

'This is stupid Inda, let us have five minutes rest and then we shall go.' they could just make out enough room to rest. The men sat down and took off their back packs.

Inda took a swig of water and began to wish that there was still whisky left, his mind was a whirl of anger, grief, and despair.

'Why can't anyone kill this bloody thing, the events that have occurred over the last few days are incredulous, Eckachandra, have you ever known anything akin to this?'

'Inda, we grew up in neighbouring villages what I know you know.'

'I cannot take it anymore I will not fear this tiger, it will fear me, I swear it.' said Inda leaping to his feet. *'I am coming for you, you hear me I am coming for you.'* he screamed into the Jungle.

Breathing heavily, his eyes red and moist, he calmed down, he listened but the jungle did not respond, not even an insect chirped acknowledgement. Sliding his back down a tree trunk he sat on the ground again sighing deeply.

'Inda, I am with you all the way but maybe it would be better for us to try and make it out of the jungle, just go home, the odds seem somewhat stacked against us.'

'I can't, I'm sorry Eckachandra, I just can't let it go, one of us must die, I know this now. We are set on a course I know not why the Gods test me so, but they have decided to do so and I will answer the call.'

'You can't think the Gods want you to die surely?'

'I have either angered them or have been chosen for something special – they are the only options that make any sense.'

'Inda I know not what this creature is, it scares me and I am not afraid to admit it.'

'Revenge is all I know now, I keep seeing the people I have failed. Charles was my employer, my friend and I let him die. I ran. I abandoned him.'

'No one holds you responsible Inda, including myself. You were preserving your own life there is no shame in that.'

'There is when your job is to ensure their safety. I have brought dishonour to my family.'

Eckachandra remained quiet, defeated, for he understood family honour.

'Well what are we going to do, what is your plan?'

'I have no plan Eckachandra just kill this thing anyway I can, let us go, the sooner we find it the sooner we can go home.'

The men got up, putting on their mudded beige canvas back packs. As they began to walk Eckachandra tripped over a log and fell to the floor.

'I have had enough of this Inda.' he said taking off his pack and going into a large side pocket that ran all the way down the side of it. Eckachandra pulled out a dark green cloth and unravelled it, the smell of paraffin filled the air as he revealed a stick with tightly wound soaked strips of cloth round the end of it.

Inda stood waiting, looking round into the darkness hoping to find his next lead. Eckachandra took a book of matches out and lit the torch, a large flame leapt from the stick and filled the jungle with orange light.

He stood up lifting the torch, pleased to see the jungle being unveiled before him. As he brought it up two neon amber stars twinkled ferociously at him, the jungle became a kaleidoscope of amber, black and orange, Inda turned round and gasped as blood spattered across his face and head, drenching him.

The torch fell to the floor, the flickering flames lit up the tiger. As it stood there in the light, the stripes on his coat came to life, the tiger's eyes glowed like orange diamonds, for a second it appeared to be some phoenix like cat made of fire.

Inda and the Tiger stood there staring intensely at each other. Eckachandra was laying there motionless in an inordinately large pool of blood.

The tiger suddenly turned. Inda immediately brought up his rifle to take a shot. He fired.

The tiger disappeared into the jungle, Inda picked up the torch and chased after him. Using the torch to light his way, he easily cleared the many obstacles of the jungle, jumping and ducking when required. He saw glimpses of orange, chasing the shadows, he slowed down and finally noticed water dripping on him, the rain was starting.

Coming to a small clearing; he threw the torch away and tore off his back pack. He grabbed some extra ammo, small food rations and a canteen of water. The small food rations he put into his pouches and filled his webbing with extra ammo, picking up the rifle and adjusting the strap he put it comfortably across his back leaving it loose enough to be easily moved round or taken off. Then he pulled out his revolver and after checking it was loaded, cocked it. Finally he pulled his large hunting knife out of its sheath.

The jungle was illuminated fluorescent green as a huge streak of lightning came down followed immediately by a crack of thunder so loud it was as if the earth itself had split in two.

Inda looked up and screamed into the sky with all his might, another crack of lightning lit him up, his face and torso doused with thick blood, there was madness in his eyes as anguish, terror and rage fought for the dominance of expression.

Inda snapped his arm out so the hunting knife was ready to strike and aimed the handgun forward, he started to run through the jungle as if he was some sort of rabid jungle man. He traversed the foliage, roots and trees at great speed as if he had placed them all there himself, his mind focused purely on vengeance. The anger and drive seemed to give him super human abilities as he ran through the terrain effortlessly. Branches and sticks nicked his limbs but he did not feel the scratches, the lightning continued unabated, getting steadily worse. The strikes became so frequent that he found himself running through a strobe lit Jungle.

Inda stopped to survey the area, 'where are you Coward, show yourself.' he said to himself as he took short sharp breaths, his eyes widened with adrenaline and determination, the sky rumbled, lightning lit the place up again, he heard the almighty roar of his foe.

Inda ran toward the direction of the roar, jumping through thick undergrowth he searched for his quarry, the flashes of lightning continued their strobe effect until at last he came upon his tormentor.

Ahead the tigers face snarled as it roared at him, but all Inda could hear was thunder - as if the tiger had roared it. Its face and body illuminated by lightning flashes as was the scar on its leg.

Inda himself was put on display, his clothes now ripped from the rushing through the thick Jungle, blood still visible but mixed with dirty rain water.

Inda held his knife up in the air and screamed. The two opponents stood there staring at each other as the rain belted down, the foliage was thin enough for them to see each other clearly. The tiger took a step forward and so did Inda. Lightning flashed again, thunder roared so loud as if all the trees had split in two.

As if by prior agreement the adversaries charged each other simultaneously. Inda ran with purpose and strength. As they approached each other the mighty cat leapt with its claws and teeth glinting in the flashes of light. Inda brought up the knife but the tiger pounced on his arm. Inda wasted no time as the cat forced him down, using its own momentum he swung it round freeing his knife arm then bringing it around for a strike, as he did the tiger swiped with its set of carving knives - both parties missed.

The tiger ran back into the jungle, Inda instinctively ran the opposite way a few paces, after quickly assessing he had no injuries other than perhaps bruises from the collision, a surge of invincibility flushed through him, he ran after the tiger.

Running into the trees flashes illuminated the orange striped ghost as it circled him, Inda bought up the handgun and let off several shots but the tiger continued to evade them. Inda emptied the gun at it, but the tiger ran through the trees as if it were passing *through* them, every shot seemed to just miss, splinters of tree bark exploded at every turn but the tiger made it and once again came charging at Inda.

The mighty beast leapt at him out of the trees, Inda tried his best to bring the knife for a straight stab through the torso but again the tiger was wily, it anticipated the move. As it landed Inda flipped the tiger again, using its own momentum in a *Judo* type throw. Inda brought the knife round and managed to slice the tiger's front shoulder but the tiger had the same idea, Inda felt searing hot pain as the set of claws tore open the flesh on his back.

The pair retreated from each other once again. Inda felt his own warm blood trickling down his back, with no way to assess how bad his injuries were he carried on. Taking the opportunity to reload the revolver Inda hoped he could end it with that as he was not sure how many encounters with this tiger he could take, if he hadn't been unknowingly killed already.

The storm raged unabated, torrential rain poured down from the sky, the thunder so loud that even when you were prepared for it you felt a pang of fear as the sky roared terribly at the earth.

As Inda walked he felt pain in his back with every step. The jungle started to thin out giving him a little more scope to see and less places for the tiger to hide. He walked around for ten minutes with the gun poised, his senses on full alert. Walking past some trees Inda instinctively turned around and fired. The bullet smashed into a tree as the tiger leapt down at him but Inda was smart he dived out of the way, spun around and took a shot narrowly missing the tigers head with his pistol.

Encouraged, Inda ran after it taking several shots as he chased it down, he soon lost it again and the game of cat and hunter resumed.

Inda seemed to have subconsciously learned its behaviour, the shot he took had been instinctive, the nestle of trees in the periphery of his gaze was the perfect territory for an ambush. Musing he realised that had he been closer his throat would have been ripped out like the shikari earlier.

The tiger tried again several times to ambush but was always thwarted by one of Inda's bullets that whilst they all missed were close enough to deter, Inda grew increasingly frustrated at his inability to hit the great cat.

The night wore on and the rain stopped, it was then that the rational side of Inda once again came to the surface, as he replayed the night's events in his mind he was shocked to discover both how brazen and how lucky he had been.

He started thinking about his new found luck and noticed that the heavy rain would cover his scent, this could greatly assist his progress. It was only then he realised that he himself was absolutely sodden, even his undergarments were soaked. His back had stopped hurting though and he was still alive. 'Must have got away with flesh wound' he thought to himself.

Inda thought carefully but did not allow fear to return, he had turned the tables on this creature. He imagined being the victor, the toast of the jungle, all the villages talking of his great adventures, passing his name down through generations.

He moved through the ever thinning jungle. The deluge of rain had been so voluminous that puddles of water and mud had collected everywhere. It was still dark but the storm had blown over, the bright silver light of the moon once again lit up the jungle floor. Inda was glad to be out of the dense jungle, despite everything that had happened through the night his rifle was still there, he took it off and after checking it returned it to its hindquarters.

Using puddles to move around he stopped to rub himself with mud. He lay down on the floor and rolled in a large puddle covering his back and front, he tore off some large leaves and stuck them strategically around his body in any place he could find. The aim was to hide his scent and break up his silhouette, albeit he was convinced that it would probably not make much difference he wanted to do everything he could.

Inda stalked the wet Jungle in silence, hoping to catch the tiger unawares. The tiger remained elusive however. Inda decided to change tact and started looking for a suitable tree where he could set up an ambush. His thinking had become strategic. He searched for a tree that he could climb with not too many ways up it.

It did not take long for him to find a suitable spot, he climbed up and managed to snuggle himself between two thick branches, it was surprisingly comfortable, he allowed himself a little respite. Inda pulled one of the energy biscuits out of his pouch and ate it. Checking his position he laid the rifle out in front of him with the strap wrapped round his arm lest he drop it. The hand gun was inspected he made sure it was secured in the holster but also that he could get to it. He decided to clip the knife back in his sheath as the last thing he wanted was to lose any of his weapons.

He aimed the gun into the jungle keeping a sharp eye out. The mud was starting to dry on his skin, he could feel dirt and grime chaffing in every orifice, he squirmed a few times but managed to get himself comfortable again. It was too comfortable. The night's events seemed like a dream. Inda did not notice or even realise that he had fallen asleep, it was a deep slumber.

An alarm call rang violently in his head, a jungle bird with an exceptionally loud, shrill had taken itself to land on his branch and cheep violently. Inda snapped awake.

The first thing he felt was the warm sun on his face, as he opened his mouth the mud pack from the previous night cracked and flaked. His eyes bleary, he forced them open wide and looked into the Jungle. The scene was beautiful and enchanting in a mesmerising way. The sun rays through the jungle slowly transformed the forest, mist hung in the air like ghostly cobwebs.

Inda could still feel the cool of the night but the sun was growing warmer by the minute. He realised that his mouth and throat were dry, thanking himself for having the prudence to bring food and water he carefully brought the canteen around from his side and took a large gulp. Allowing it to go down he took another, then screwed the lid back on and swung the canteen back to its position. The rifle was laying on the branch still attached to his hand, for the first time the tiger entered his mind, he wondered what game it was playing now.

Thinking about what his next move would be Inda realised how much his body ached. It throbbed everywhere - his back was sore. He slowly pushed himself up onto all fours, wincing as he did. Slowly he sat back against the main trunk. He looked down and nearly fell off the branch. At the base of the tree the tiger sat swishing its tail and licking its lips.

Inda immediately went for his revolver as soon as he did the tiger turned to run but the jungle had thinned out. Inda fired rapidly, several bullets danced at the tiger's feet causing it to change course. Inda scrambled out of the tree as fast as he could jumping down with the rifle in one hand and the handgun in the other. He started to run slinging the rifle over his back and reloading the handgun as he did.

The tiger quickly outran him. Inda could not help but admire how fast and easily his adversary could hide. Slowing down Inda gathered his senses, there was still plenty of mud and water, he remembered his plan and started walking in water and mud wherever possible. He noticed a tree leaking out sweet smelling sap, he covered his shoes in it, walking slowly he skulked through the now forest for forty minutes without coming across his mighty opponent.

Feeling exasperated Inda stopped for a drink and leant against a large trunk allowing himself to gaze aimlessly for a second at a large puddle set in a cauldron of mud. Then he realised what he was looking at, in the mud was the track of a very large male tiger. Inda beamed to himself. 'I have you now my friend.'

Immediately he swapped weapons putting the gun back in its leather pouch pulling around the rifle making sure it was primed. Inspecting the tracks Inda determined that they were very fresh. He crept along, stopping every few minutes to scan ahead for a shot, but to no avail. He followed the tracks for about fifteen minutes before losing them.

He walked for five minutes then returned to the same point where he had lost the tracks, he did this several times, each time heading off in a different direction from the point of origin. The extensive research paid off, he managed to find a sign, then some paw prints. Back on the trail he carried on using water and mud wherever he could. There was long grass up ahead, as he approached the tree line he checked up in the trees.

As Inda went to walk into the field of long grass he paused, instead he began walking around the periphery 'I'm not falling for that trap,' he thought to himself. Not seeing anything he continued walking. Inda noticed the grass tops move slightly out of synch, he tiptoed closer but could not see through the grass, so he ran around the field as quietly as he could to find another angle. The grass thinned out towards the rear of the field, Inda managed to find a gap.

He trained his rifle, through the grass he could see the tiger. It was big.

Inda smiled, getting down on one knee he took a deep breath and aimed. He studied the tiger, where it was breathing, he tried to breath with it, he wanted to hit his target exactly, to end it with one shot. Savouring his victory Inda licked his lips, his finger on the trigger he gently started to squeeze, as he did something occurred to him, the scar on its front leg – where was it? And surely it should have one on the shoulder now as well?

'Oh no.' said Inda as he turned his head just in time to see the claw rip half of his face off with one swipe. He could just make out his opponents giant teeth as he heard a loud slushy crunch and his lights went out.

~

Adjacent to the old colonial hotel stood a piece of land in the shape of a large oval; a makeshift fence stood marking its perimeter. The fence was made out of crudely cut logs, as you walked in a large courtyard greeted you, at the end of which sat a giant canvas marquee with large tents dotted either side of it and several Rolls Royce's were parked down one side. The sun was high in the sky, the mud of the courtyard was bone dry already, there was no sign of last night's storm.

It was obvious that this was a makeshift camp, albeit one of opulence. You could be mistaken for thinking as you entered the main marquee that some sheik or super wealthy foreign dignitary was visiting. Fine silks hung from the walls, a gargantuan Arabic rug filled the room. Gold fixtures, lamps and expensive antique looking sideboards accompanied the bar that ran down one side. A wall of thick maroon velvet ran along the back wall beyond which were sleeping quarters and a luxurious bathroom complete with marble flooring. Large gold ceiling fans hung from makeshift wooden beams.

Two huge portions of the tent rolled back to open up the front of this giant marquee. Toward the back of the room in the centre was a large throne like chair facing the wide open entrance.

The man with reddish ginger hair sat in silence enjoying the mixture of cool and warmth as the heat from outside battled the breeze of the fans. The sun was shining bright, plants and grass were evident throughout the courtyard but constantly fighting a losing war against the tide of footsteps and vehicles that traversed it.

But in bright sunlight there is little that doesn't seem somehow beautiful. The man with florid cheeks sat with a bottle of whisky next to him along with a bucket of freshly delivered ice. The whisky was extremely expensive and very familiar as it was the same bottle Charles had been drinking the morning he set out to catch the male tiger.

The man picked up his glass and sipped the extravagant firewater not taking his eyes off the door while he did. Such was his concentration that he did not even hear the man approach him from behind.

'Sir, what is it?' said the Indian man with longish black hair and a well-kept beard that helped hide a potted face, he also wore a white tunic.

'Vallabhendra, it's George, call me George confound you, you're as much my friend as you are my employee and you're certainly not my slave.'

'Very well, apologies, George.' Vallabhendra replied.

George rolled his eyes in despair. 'What is it anyway?' George asked, now rather annoyed.

'Sir ... I mean George, forgive my intrusion but what disturbs you so, you have been staring at that doorway for two hours, what is you wait for?'

George threw a couple more cubes into his nearly empty glass and poured another generous helping of the illustrious firewater. Staring out into the sun he brought the glass to his lips listening to the ice crack as he did. He felt the warmth slide down his gullet and into his stomach, exhaling deeply he said. 'I am waiting for he who comes.'

'I do not understand, to whom do you refer?'

'To whom, your English is better than mine Vallabhendra. There are some things you cannot escape, some things cannot be outran, sometimes you know what is to come.'

Vallabhendra scratched his head and went to speak, but George held up his hand.

'You will understand soon enough.' said George not taking his eyes off the doorway.

'I shall leave you ... call if you want me Sir ... uh ... George.'

'Thanks, will do.' replied George.

Vallabhendra retreated as silently as he had arrived.

George sat there for about twenty minutes in a deep trance. He finished his glass of whisky and slowly poured himself another from the bottle right next to him, as he looked back toward the doorway a huge tiger walked into view.

George took a sip from his glass, swirling the drink and rattling the ice as he did. The tiger stood in the doorway and stared at him, it still had the scar down it's leg which made it so identifiable but as well as that there was a fresh scar on its shoulder, a knife wound, it was apparent yet superficial.

'I have been waiting for you, I wondered when you would come.' George said keeping eye contact with his trespasser. 'But I knew you would.' continued George holding his drink up to the great cat.

George heard a slight noise from behind and sensed that Vallabhendra had appeared from behind the curtain. He waved him back and heard the curtain swish as Vallabhendra disappeared, the whole time George never took his eye off the tiger.

The great cat stepped forward, George could see it in all its glory, he was sure he had never seen a tiger been so big. As it walked its bulging muscles flexed, it had dried blood around its mouth. It stopped just inside the tent.

George remained stoical. 'Why do you wait?' he asked.

The tiger crept slowly forward swishing its tail and licking its lips, George sat there watching it approach, he took another sip of whisky then put the glass back on the small table next to him.

Suddenly the tiger charged and jumped on him, the weight of the cat's front paws was incredible, George immediately grabbed its head from either side and ruffled its fur.

'Did those nasty men try to hurt you? Did they? Did they?' The tiger started licking George's face and tried to jump completely on him.

'You can't sit on my knee you great oaf.' said George pushing the tiger down again. The cat nuzzled its head against his legs, George kept on fussing it. He grabbed his glass and finished the rest of it in one gulp, putting the tumbler back on the table, he walked out with the tiger walking by his side.

Outside the sun's heat hit with force, the tiger let out an almighty roar instantly causing a great commotion.

Birds, monkeys, kakar panicked and fled, rumbling filled the air like war drums being played before a battle as tigers ran up over the fence from all directions. A multitude of giant cats filled the large arena, they roared in unison - a thousand thunderstorms and volcanoes erupting all at once. The ground shook, creatures of all varieties evacuated in a petrified state.

Animals cried out in alarm and fear, a woman came out onto the balcony of the hotel and screamed with all her might. Several men ran out onto the balcony with guns but upon seeing a courtyard full of ferocious and vengeful cats they threw their guns away and jumped over the balcony in panic.

The roars continued, people started jumping out of windows as tigers filled the hotel, a woman's body flew out of one of the upstairs windows, flames erupted out of a window downstairs, people ran everywhere screaming and shouting in blind panic, several pointless gun shots were heard, tyres screeched.

'Perhaps this cat of yours really was sent by a spirit.' said Vallabhendra.

'Or maybe it is just Nature's Payback.' responded George.

The tigers filled the arena; they all lay down leaving a parting down the middle leading from the marquee to the main gates.

Vallabhendra came out of the huge tent and stood waiting patiently behind George and the tiger, George turned and gave him a look. Vallabhendra stepped forward so he was standing beside them. Together they began to walk down the centre.

'At last, the Jungle is back in the hands of its rightful owners.' said George.

Tiger! Tiger! Tiger!

Volume III

The Great Tiger King

Years had passed since the events of Charles and Inda. The great striped cats had taken over and now deep in the jungle a kingdom of tigers had been established. George and Vallabhendra ruled as kings. There were no fences or walls, no guards to keep people out, only the tigers themselves. No one ventured forth, no one except the invited and even they were reticent, most turned back in sheer terror.

Many people came near, daring each other to try and catch a glimpse of the now famed cats or their infamous masters, they had all quickly passed in to Indian folklore. There was but one road that led in to the compound and it swarmed with man eaters or so it was said. Not just any kind of man eating tiger, these tigers could read your soul, they knew your intentions, if you ventured forth with an impure heart you would be devoured by a striped judge.

Rumours abounded that the two men sat like kings on twin thrones in a courtyard full of tigers eating raw meat provided to them by the felines, so attuned were they that they spoke and even walked like tigers, as far from as human as could be and as near as cat as possible.

As for the truth …

The tent still stood, nothing appeared worn, even the tapestries that hung had not aged, the furnishing replaced when needed. The fence compiled of large logs had gone, all sawn down to the height of a man's knee so it was easy for anyone or thing to enter. The entrance was still in the same location but gone were the intimidating gates now nothing but a large gap in the low cut fence.

The hotel long since abandoned had been saved and restored, sitting in all its splendour it stood defiant to its surroundings and the feline revolution. The bar was as it was before, George and Vallabhendra still frequented it, especially George and especially when he desired to reminisce.

The left wing downstairs was occupied by tigers and used as shelter for the old or injured. The right wing which housed the bar was used for honoured guests and dignitaries as well as some staff.

It was not quite true that anyone who was not deemed worthy would be killed. It has been said by many people that George would bring a tiger usually the one with the scar down its leg and if the tiger took a disliking to them they would be escorted to the edge of the kingdom by George himself and released without harm. There are many people who attest to this and claim to be one of them. It may be noted however that very few people have made it or even claimed to have made it as far as the compound, the hearth of the Tiger Kingdom.

They were not thrones, just old dining chairs from Tudor Times that had been shipped in, it was the lavish red upholstery added for comfort and the oversized arms that gave them the appearance of thrones.

The tent doors wide open, a warm breeze gently blowing in, you could hear the milling about of both tiger and man in the courtyard outside. A truck pulled up and a man got out, he was instantly surrounded by tigers, one or two tugged at his clothes while another jumped up, he pushed it off but it still kept trying to jump up and lick him.

The whisky bottle sat on a fine looking antique table that was placed between the chairs, an ice bucket stood either side always full even in the heat of summer. The man in khaki shorts sat inside the huge tent watching the supply truck arrive. Men were grabbing boxes tied together with rope and pointing to different store areas, the tigers took the parcels and dropped them in the designated area.

The place was abuzz with both man and tiger, the hotel stood in grand gesture to its occupants, the land at peace, the true kings of the jungle had arrived and tigers ruled all they surveyed.

This land of hope and claw, so feared, was for a while loved by all.

Next to the throne like chairs were slightly smaller guest chairs but just as eloquent.

'You came here to talk about your father I presume?'

'That is correct Sir.'

'Please, call me George.'

'Very well George, thank you for seeing me, I am glad you received my letter. You are my last chance to uncover the truth, I know you did not know my father well. Before we begin let me state that I in no way at all hold you or your cat responsible.'

'Pleased to hear it.' said George picking up his glass and taking a sip whilst eyeing his interlocutor with curiosity.

'My name is Jayadev, my father was Arshad, he died in the ill fated tiger hunt in which you participated I understand.'

'Yes I abandoned the party, the outcome was inevitable ... blast their confounded ways if only they had listened to me.' Moistness shot into George's eyes as deceased faces flashed through his mind.

'Forgive me George I see that it has bought you great pain also.'

'Well there is nothing that can be done now, tell me what exactly is it that you want to know, your letter was vague.'

'Purposefully so I'm afraid, I wanted to meet you, you and your land of tigers have become legendary throughout India, people have even started making pilgrimages just to see your borders.'

'First, this land belongs to the tiger and to Mother India, but if I were to claim to ownership it just as much belongs to Vallabhendra.'

'Of course you are all famous - the kings of India they call you, for you speak to the tiger and thus rule this land along with the great tiger king.'

George raised his eyebrows in surprise.

'The tiger itself, the one sent by a God or Goddess is considered to be the king supreme. King of Man, King of Cats and King of all India – The Great Tiger King.'

'Yes, there a lot of links to tigers in different faiths if I am not mistaken.'

Jayadev looked impressed and nodded slightly before answering. 'You surprise me George visitors to our shores tend not to pay any attention to our customs and certainly not to our beliefs.'

'That's because their bloody rude.' George answered hotly.

Jayadev gave the briefest of sniggers, more like a half murdered snort. 'Please do not be fooled sir, if one of our deities appeared to you, you would surely die of fright.'

'I'm sure I would old man.' said George leaning back and taking a large swig of his whisky.

'The Great Tiger King.' said Jayadev to himself and also taking a drink.

George Guffawed. 'Has it really come to this, The Great Tiger King?'

'Do you not read the papers?'

'Yes, I hadn't realised the rumours had pervaded *all* of India.'

'Yes, you have entered folklore already sahib.'

'Such nonsense,' said George dismissing it with his hand.

'Now, what was it that you wanted to know about your father?'

Jayadev put his glass down on the small table next to him and leant forward. 'I just want to know how he died, well any specifics you may know. I understand you tracked after them the next day with a party and you were the one who found their bodies.'

'Look you will have to forgive me Jayadev, but who exactly was your father?'

'I believe he was found by a campfire.'

'Oh right.' George said solemnly, turning to the table and refilling his glass, he noticed that the talisman on a leather strap around his guest's neck was Jade.

'Yes I remember him, did he carry a jade miniature statue of a goddess around with him in a green cloth?'

'Yes, yes he did.' his face read excitement for a second but then despair.

'Yes I was the one who found him, your father died with great dignity and an immeasurable amount of honour.'

'In what way?'

'I examined the scene for albeit we know what killed them the details could still be of interest. The first thing I noticed was that his weapons were not on him. They were on the ground nearby, not that close though.'

'Why on earth did he not have his weapons to hand?' said Jayadev leaning even closer.

George softened his eyes and rubbed his chin slightly.

'I examined the tracks around him, there was no struggle of any kind, just the tracks of Alistair going to take his fated place on the rocks after Inda had presumably given chase. The statue I informed you of wasn't in his pocket, it was on display with burnt josticks either side of it, your father had removed all of his webbing, even his utility belt and shirt.'

'You mean ... he sacrificed himself.' said Jayadev startled.

'That is exactly what I mean, it was obvious that his weapons had been thrown and not dropped.'

'You see - already I am glad I sought you out George, now I can celebrate my Father's death and hope to have his courage.'

'He certainly seems to have died with incredible dignity, the tiger being so highly regarded in India is no mistake, it is the mightiest, most glorious creature on the face of this earth, I kid you not and confound the men that do not see it. So what do you think of the place?'

'Impressed and astounded are the words I would choose. How do you manage to keep to the tigers at bay?'

'We do not, that is the point, they are free animals, we do not own them so they wonder free.'

'But they obey you do they not?'

'Well yes, in ways, but they are not forced to and believe or it not they often feed *us*.'

'You jest, surely.'

'I assure you I do not Sir, you must have tried deer at some point have you not?'

'Once, naturally killed, it was very tasty.'

'Well you know what the tiger eats, is it so strange that it brings meat home, even the domestic cat does that.'

His interlocutor laughed nervously. 'Why I suppose you are right, do you eat the meat raw?'

'Don't be so bloody ridiculous what do you take me for a savage?'

'Apologies I had no intention of offending my host.'

'The only offence is asking such a stupid question.'

'Right again I fear Sahib.' Jayadev replied.

'Think of it as a community of like minded beings, all we want to do is live in peace and why not, the jungle is a beautiful place.'

'*That* I understand, thank you again fo ...'

Jayadev fell silent, his longish black hair seem to freeze along with his body, the pallor of his skin paled rapidly, his mouth fell agape, his eyes opened wide with terror.

Astonished George watched his interlocutor fix his gaze across the room. With both men not talking and no sound coming from outside (a rarity which under any other circumstance George absolutely treasured), a loud, deep, gasping, growling sound filled the room.

The man lifted his shaking hand and pointed, 'it's him isn't it, it's him, the one, the judge of mankind, the slayer of inequity.'

George turned his head to see his beloved tiger on the floor fast asleep.

'It looks so big, the ...'

The ominous sound stopped without warning, Jayadev looked too frightened to speak, he clutched at a jade talisman around his neck.

'No please ... no ...'

As if the tiger had heard him talk, it stirred from its sleep, instantly rose and started walking towards him.

'That is the biggest cat that ever lived I assure you.' he said breathing in sharply like someone who had just jumped into a pool of freezing cold water. 'The scar on its leg, it is him, it is the one, the one who can't be killed, the one who comes again.'

George looked at the Tigers scar on its leg which now looked like a long grey pencil line.

Jayadev was still breathing short sharp breaths of deep panic. 'But it can't be, he hasn't aged, it looks still in its prime, it is must be the oldest cat in history.'

'Alright old boy calm down, it won't hurt you I promise.'

'Please stop it Sahib I beg you.'

The muscular tiger with its huge bulk strode forward slowly with determination, Jayadev started to pray, he could have sworn that the ground shook with every step.

The tiger walking right in front of George finally reached its destination. Even sitting down the tiger's head was a lot bigger than Jayadev's torso. Sweating with fear he started praying feverishly with his hands. The tiger looked into his eye's, Jayadev could not help but look back. The head of the tiger came forward, up over the knees towards his face and chest.

'*Sahib please.*' he shrieked in a shrill whisper, but George remained silent. The tiger suddenly jumped its two front legs up onto the chair's arms, rising on its two hind legs the huge beast towered over him.

George saw on Jayadev a face that he had seen all too many times in his life and one that he did not particularly care to see again, it was the face of a man preparing to die. Resignation leapt across Jayadev's face like a black cat across someone's path, he had accepted that he was to die.

The tiger leant in deliciously slowly, Jayadev tried to rear his face away as much he could, George watched him trying to avoid the hot stench of the tigers breath.

The teeth came lower and lower, the mouth slowly started to open, it got right to his face and then gently licked him.

As the tiger swiftly returned to its former position in front of him, relief and joy burst from Jayadev's face. 'I passed, I passed.' he said.

'Yes you did but as I said you were quite safe, if you had not, he would not have licked you but sat back down and growled at you, then I would have sent him back to his bed, gave you five minutes conversation out of courtesy, then personally escorted you out of the kingdom.'

'I think I'll have another drink now Sahib.'

George let out a loud guffaw. 'I thought you might old man.' George leant forward in a most eager manner and poured a generous helping of whisky. He gave the glass to his guest, the ice rattled boisterously as the man pulled the glass to his chest and exhaled relief from the pit of his stomach.

'There is nothing to fear now, I promise you that much.' George said noticing that the man's hand was trembling causing the ice to continuously rattle. He looked at his guest he was a good looking man. George approximated he was in his late twenties, he had shiny black hair that came down to his shoulders.

'A magnificent beast, I thought I was ready but upon seeing it up close, even being in the same room as it ... I think those who seek it will immediately regret it once their eyes fall upon him.' Jayadev said readjusting his position, sitting upright. He spread his arms out a little and puffed up his chest.

George picked up his drink, took a huge gulp, letting the whisky burn his mouth some before he swallowed it.

Then George himself exhaled deeply, he looked at his beloved tiger now laying on the floor in front of the two thrones, the tiger was still facing their guest.

'It's funny all that has transpired, so many think of him as some mystical being or divine creation, but to me he's just my cat.'

Jayadev who was sipping down his firewater choked upon hearing this, but upon George ignoring the involuntary gesture he remained silent.

George took the whisky bottle and filled his glass even though it was already half full, he gestured but his guest refused.

'It was after the Great War that I decided to come to India. I fought and led in the trenches and won many medals, including the Victoria Cross. I saw so many people die, including many close personal friends, but it is the men I killed that seem to haunt me the most. I regret to say but I even killed the innocent, not intentionally you understand but in the vague blood spattered heat of battle sometimes you can't tell what is what.

I was called a hero and received many a pat on the back but I could not adjust to life in old blighty again, even though I wanted to. The same trees, the same looking fields, even the same faces, much of Europe looks the same; within reason anyway and before battle of course.

Money was not an issue to me, I came from good stock, born into money and title as it were, we have never been people to shy away from what's needed and if my country required it then I would be there.

I soon realised that the impact of war had changed my life forever, a friend of mine who happens to be a doctor suggested that I get a complete change of scene. My uncle lived out here, we get on particularly well, I wrote to him and within a month I was in India.'

George looked up for a moment, his guest sensing he was about to change the subject quickly intervened.

'Please Sahib continue I am most intrigued and honoured that you would relate your history with me.'

George looked at him for a second and after gulping half of his glass down continued his discourse.

'My uncle had taken to life in India, living half in the wilds. I was enamoured instantly and knew I had found my place of restitution. The wild plants and animals enchanted me from the start. Helping my uncle with day to day life I soon settled down, the scars began to heal, the memories dissipated some, the ghosts became more controllable.

You must understand I never really gave India much thought before The Great War. I was aware of it especially as my uncle had moved there but I did not pay much attention, I had also heard that there were tigers but my attitude was again nonchalant. I clearly remember the first time my uncle mentioned tigers to me, I believe it was the evening of my first day and I, having arrived early in the morning was sitting on some safari like chairs in the grass in front of his house.

He told me that the only real danger that one had to face out here were tigers and the occasional leopard. The truth be told I was not frightened at all, after the experience of war, I gained a somewhat irrational loss of fear. I remember in the first few weeks I was curious to see a tiger after hearing about them again from locals, I even went looking for one on my own, I was unarmed as well.

'What happened?' asked Jayadev leaning forward placing his glass on the table next to him.

'Nothing actually,' said George 'I did not see one, it was many months before I eventually met the great oaf.'

Upon saying that George using his feet gently nudged the tiger in its side whilst it was trying to sleep, the great cat lifted its giant head and growled. Jayadev sat back. George leant down towards the tiger and snarled back, grimacing his teeth and growling as loud as he could from the back of his throat. The tiger looked almost bemused, Jayadev could have sworn he saw the cat roll its eyes as it put its head back on its paws which were so big they seemed like two large bouncy orange cushions.

'I was walking through the jungle one day when I heard a twig snap. I stopped and listened and heard the jungle foliage being gently and softly trampled on, I suspected it could be some native wildlife that I hadn't yet stumbled upon, I had in mind a deer or even a wild boar never in my wildest dreams did I imagine I was walking straight towards a tiger!

As it happens I wasn't, I was walking straight towards two. Brushing aside the leaves and branches I expected at any moment to hear the tumultuous commotion of a sizeable creature running for its life as it heard me clodhopping through the rain forest like an elephant in a glassware store.

Coming to a little clearing I immediately saw a cub coiled back, growling at me fiercely, ready to pounce. I was not without caution for it was quite grown, probably about fifteen or sixteen months old, I was pretty sure it already knew how to hunt, and if knew how to hunt then it knew how to attack. Albeit distracted I could see the reason for its defensiveness, why he hadn't ran. Next to him was a huge tigress, with blood pouring from her chest, she had been shot, by a poacher I suspect.

Without going into greater detail and at the risk of enjoying the sound of my own voice, let me just state that there was a tense standoff. I could see the tigress laying with her tongue hanging out panting, I pulled out my canteen of water and eventually managed to persuade the young tiger to allow me near its mother. I gently poured the water in her mouth and watched as she lapped it up with a look of relief that I will never forget. As strange as it may seem although it was a cat, I saw the faces of a thousand dying men from my Great War.

The cub seemed to relax. I had some food upon me, a habit I suppose to carry some kind of ration with me. I fed the mother and gave a tiny bit to the cub, sensing that I had earned their trust I motioned for them to stay there and ran back to the house where I collected some people. It was nearly night by the time we managed to stretcher the mother back to my abode. We collected bundles of grass and hay then placed them in the corner of the main room. The men were too frightened to stay in the house, but a vet attended and decided to stay the course with me. Looking back I am astounded that it all happened, but I suppose I didn't really think about it, a job had to be done, so I did it.

The tigress, began to recover some after a few days. Despite being fed, the cub started running off into the jungle for hours at a time and then returning. Letting himself in as if he was a normal domestic cat.

On one of these trips, the minute the young tiger had left for the jungle we quickly knocked out the tigress and removed the bullet. After that she started to recover to the point of getting up and walking around again much to the cub's delight, but the tigress never strayed far, it was as if she knew she was safe there.

My uncle it might be said was less than impressed by all these feline shenanigans, he protested some but largely remained stoical as was his way.

One morning a week or so I later I got up and went downstairs, the tigress was back laying on her sick bed and immediately I knew something was wrong, my gut told me there was nothing that could be done, I could see my old friend the spectre of death had to come to visit my world yet again.

The vet hurried over, he had since cut back on his time as the tigress had been recovering well. After an examination at which neither the tigress nor the cub protested at he looked at me and shook his head. He explained that unbeknownst to us an infection had set in and completely taken hold and that it probably wouldn't be long.

We sat up all night with the tigress, I had started becoming friendly with the cub, it now let me stroke and play with it.

But that night the cub just lay there moping, a couple of times it got up and tried to comfort its mother but she was too weak to respond with the exception of a quick nod or brief raise of her head. The humane thing to do would have been to shoot her in the head, but I did not want to traumatise the youngster for I had gained his trust and I sensed he knew what was about to pass.'

George leaned over and refilled his glass with both ice and firewater, he motioned towards Jayadev who upon recognising the serious stare indicated it be rude not to, offered his glass.

George sat back and took a sip. Breathing deeply again he looked at the cat without giving much eye contact to his guest at all.

'We stayed up all night, made the tigress as comfortable as we could, but in the early hours the large belly stopped rising and she breathed her last. I will never forget the young tiger letting out a yelp as she passed and to this day I wake up in the night dreaming of it, it's funny how things stay with a man.'

'Yes it is *sahib*.' said Jayadev.

'I left some food and water out for the tiger and retired to bed. The next morning when I awoke the cat was still there by its mother. I left it until the afternoon and upon deciding that it had grieved long enough, I took the tigress a way down the field and buried her. The youngster never once left my side, when I had finished I said a small prayer, to this day I have no idea what possessed me, I am a man of faith but praying for a cat to make show for cat is quite beyond my logic. I guess I was beginning to see that young tiger as a surrogate son. I really should slow this drinking.' said George raising his glass and eyeing it suspiciously as if it had just betrayed him.

'You have me hooked sir you cannot possibly leave me hanging now.' Jayadev said shifting uncomfortably.

'Very well, the tiger fled into the jungle after that but as I sat in my parlour room nearing dusk, the tiger returned and sat in my doorway. I welcomed him but he stayed put. Getting up I cleared his mother's bedding and put it in a pile out the back to be burned. I cleaned and scrubbed the area, brought in a small section of a log for him to scratch his claws and plumped up a fresh load of grassy straw to make him a comfortable bed, I motioned to it but he just stood there. After looking he motioned to the jungle with his head. My heart sank for I knew straight away what he wanted, he wanted to be wild, who was I to stand in the way of that? I remember watching him walk slowly off to the jungle that bordered the property, I stood there in the doorway my arm leaning on the frame watching him. Just before he entered the jungle he turned, gave me one last look and disappeared.

I tried to put the whole thing out of my mind but that tiger had somehow captured my soul, I worried about him desperately, should the doctor not have popped by and instilled some wise counsel I believe I would have tried to track him that night. I am a man and a man I shall be, so I retired that night deciding not to think about the young tiger anymore unless it was a pleasant memory.

The sight that greeted me that morning was ghastly, right on my doorstep was a pool of blood, in the middle of which was a young sambar deer. Quickly I realised this was killed by my tiger as a present or thank you, I leapt over the carcass running a short distance in to the grass hoping to see my friend once again, he was nowhere to be seen.

I returned to the house heavy hearted, pondering how to clean all the blood up. As I entered my abode the tiger was sitting in the middle of the room looking at me incredulously as if to say who are you are looking for? He leapt up at me as I approached, naturally I made a fuss of him, then he went over and laid in the bed. I put out some food and water - that is where it all started.'

'So he could fend for himself then?' asked Jayadev sitting upright.

'Yes very much so, he was almost an adult, as I said the young ones stay with their mothers for anywhere up to two years. I became glad of his age as I quickly realised that he was two thirds wild and a third tame. He would still go out, hunt, mark his territory, but as it grew up I taught it to fear all man apart from me, we used to play hide and seek in the house, then we moved it into the grass, but when he became fully grown we would play at it in the jungle. That cat knows man, inside every trick, I even showed him traps. In return he taught me just how cunning and guile the tiger was, he would never fail to find me in minutes even when I crossed water and tried a dozen other tricks.

Sometimes when I would be trying to seek him he would just be following me the whole time, I would cry out in exasperation and he would step out of a bush right behind me or something.

One peculiar side effect was that I took quite a liking to deer, he would always bring me some of his kill, at first I was reticent but as it was fresh when he brought it I thought why not? You see that brown coat over there?'

'Yes.'

'That is made out of the deer he bought me on that very first day after his mother had died.'

'A memento?' Jayadev asked?

'Yes, something of that nature, I knew from that moment that our lives would be entwined and I was destined to spend the rest of my days in India. It was confirmed after the tiger was fully grown when my uncle died, my family in England begged me to return but my uncle had left me all his property and Mother India had me wrapped in her bosom.

A few years passed when one day the house mysteriously caught fire, I say mysteriously it was those bloody poachers with whom I had had a fracas with a few days earlier ... *confound the blasted rascals* ... I should have asked you to deal with them shouldn't I?' George said hotly leaning down speaking to the tiger with flushed cheeks, the tiger just ignored him.

It all burnt to the ground, but while I owned plenty of land I didn't have that many buildings on it. In the bar that night at the hotel the then proprietor offered me the outpost next door which had been abandoned about six months prior and was now used mainly for storage. I was quick to refuse but he pointed out how much it suited my lifestyle.

Half reluctant yet half curious I agreed to have a look, although the place had fallen into disrepair I immediately saw its potential. Agreeing to take it on I started work straight away, cutting a gap in the fence at the back as I knew the tiger would seek me out. I do not worry about him finding me, I purposefully shooed him off when he came to investigate the fire at my uncle's house as I knew it would attract people and if he was spotted they would hunt him.

It turned out it was my very first night when he visited, I hung the sweaty clothes I had been wearing all day on the back of the fence, adjacent to the hole so he could trace my scent if needs be. Late into the evening I heard branches breaking and bracken being pushed aside and in he strode. From then on things continued as normal for quite a while, of course there were many close shaves, it roared one time and some people near the hotel heard. I managed to persuade the proprietor the next day it was me practicing my call for hunting.

And so a few years passed. One morning I was greeted by two tigers, they were snuggled up like a couple of teenagers, I had to laugh, it seemed my cat had found himself a girlfriend. She was a bit nervous about meeting me and if it weren't for him I would have surely been attacked. I gave them both some food, she soon warmed to me. They would come by and visit often. It seems odd knowing tiger's mating rituals, they acted more like humans, they used to play in the long grass together and chase each other around, I tell you Jayadev they were just like a couple of teenagers.

This continued for a couple of months. I was already growing concerned as the tigress had now taken me into her confidence, it was inevitable that they would soon have a litter and they knew where the safest place for their cubs was. The situation would quickly become unmanageable, how my secret had held out as long it had I will never know, for one thing I was endlessly quizzed about my constant supply of deer when they never saw me go out hunting.

I will never forget that fateful day, I was sitting in my chair reading as I often like to do, when I heard my tiger call. The call was unlike any I had ever heard; it seemed full of anguish and pain. In an instant I ran out of the back of my tent and saw my tiger in anguish with blood round his mouth and a long open gash in his left leg. I called him over as I wanted to tend to his wound, but he was inconsolable, raging and pacing he attacked a tree and nearly brought the bloody thing down.

I feel rather obtuse now that I did not figure out immediately what had happened. The tigress suddenly flashed into my mind and I wondered if something had happened to her, it would explain his rage, as you are probably aware a tiger in heat can be one of the most dangerous creatures on the whole planet.

The tiger went to walk away into the jungle, I got vexed with him out of worry and bellowing at the top of my voice I commanded him to come back. He stopped and looking briefly back at me, he roared another anguished cry then headed back into the jungle.

Later on that day I heard about Charles' adventure and knew my life was about to change dramatically yet again.

The problem was I could not find my tiger before the meeting with Charles and it would have been mighty suspicious to not accompany him. I was going to knock Charles off his shot – I considered relating my whole story to him but after it started killing I knew this would do no good they would be forever convinced it was a man-eater and just for the record I still do not consider it to be.'

'That is quite an extraordinary remark if you don't mind me saying George.'

'Yes it must seem a bizarre statement, but I am telling you it was revenge, plain and simple. The only people it killed were hunting it and as far as the tiger was concerned they had killed his true love - of that I am sure. It might sound odd but I charge you to prove otherwise, why has it been near my side ever since? Why does it restrain if it does not like or approve of visitors?'

'I see your argument, Sahib.'

George intentionally cleared his throat.

'Sorry, I see your argument *George.*'

'My thinking was when I first left Charles I could continue looking for the tiger myself and that was what I did. Much to Gerald's chagrin I jumped out of the vehicle down the road and began tracking, before I could catch up with him I came across what was left of Charles. Obviously my first reaction was scoop the leftover fragments of his body up and head back to report it but my instinct told me to leave it be and play completely ignorant lest any suspicion fall upon me.

I had already experienced one close encounter while tracking them, I heard a loud commotion, something coming through the jungle at immense speed, barging through the undergrowth. For a minute I thought it might have been my cat and stood there waiting to greet to it, just in time I realised it was a man and not just any man, it was Inda fleeing the hunt. I quickly darted behind a large tree, he was in such a rush that he ran right past me. My biggest fear of course was being caught in the open with my tiger and thus it being realised that it was *my* tiger.

Things spiralled out of control once I got back. After discovering Charles, I sat awaiting for the tiger to return hoping that his thirst for blood had been sated. When he didn't show I was suspicious that this was not over. As soon as Charles was discovered a massive hunt would begin and as my tiger was not responding to me I was quite powerless. I sat up all night thinking of a plausible reason to call off the hunt and while I thought of a few, none were good enough to deter the fury of man.

I decided to myself the only real chance I had was to join the pack and act oblivious to what had transpired. I informed Gerald I hadn't found anything then acted shocked at the news about Charles. Please do not misunderstand my actions as callous or that I am without candour, on the contrary, I miss my friends more than anyone.

There was nothing I could do, it was not as if I had the tiger on a leash or had set it on them. It was the tiger's choice. As the second hunt began I sensed the true gravity of the situation. The best thing anyone could do was to leave the cat alone to grieve, but they would not listen.

Remember I told you previously that he used to track me through the jungle? When people started getting killed right under my nose, I knew he would not stop, if you hunted him or his wife – he hunted you.

To retreat from the hunt was the only viable option. If they all returned to the hotel they would be safe. Left for a few days it would have been avoided as my tiger would sought me out sooner or later and it wouldn't have been that long no matter what the circumstance. The second and most vital point was the fact that the tiger was so used to tracking me that effectively me being in the party was acting like a tracking beacon. I was effectively marching the men to their deaths, but the men would not return with me. When the great tiger returned he brought all his friends with him (assumedly for protection) and so this land of tigers was born.'

'There is one thing that I do not understand.' said Jayadev, now looking more composed in his host's company even with the giant tiger still at his feet.

'What is that, speak man.' said George sitting up in anticipation.

'Why did you never give him a name?' asked Jayadev motioning toward the tiger with his glass.

'That is a good question ...' George put his now empty glass on the table next to him and thought about it for a minute. 'As much as he was my pet and part of my household, I wanted him to keep his freedom. I encouraged him to be wild, to roam free. As peculiar a statement as it maybe, giving him a name would dishonour that, he is the true king of the jungle and as if that is his title I don't see why he needs a name.'

'I want to say to you George never have I met an Englishman with such an understanding of our country and it's spirit.'

George laughed out loud, 'We're not all bad you know.'

'I see that now.' said jayadev smiling warmly.

The curtain at the back swished violently open and Vallabhendra came striding in. He was a large man, tall and muscular. His hair was scruffy and shorter than before, it no longer reached his shoulders. He still had a big black beard which now completely hid his potholed complexion. Vallabhendra was sporting a light sandy coloured uniform that was akin to the Indian army, he also wore a ceremonial dagger on his side.

'Vallabhendra meet Jayadev, this is the gentleman I was telling you about who wrote me a letter.'

'I see, pleased to meet you, you are most welcome.'

Jayadev went to get up but realising the tiger was resting, cautiously sat back down.

Vallabhendra bellowed out a great laugh. 'Don't worry about him he is just a harmless pussy cat.'

Jayadev had look of incredulity painted across his face.

'Aren't you, hey, a big harmless pussy cat, hey?'

Vallabhendra lightly kicked the cat in the back leg. A low rumble emitted from the tigers gullet.

'Oi, I am talking to you.' said Vallabhendra shoving the cat with his foot. 'Don't ignore me.' The growl got deeper and louder.

'Please Vallabhendra I beseech you do not make it angry, I do not fancy being on his menu today.'

'Nonsense Jayadev he's just a pussy cat aren't you, what are you going to do hey?' said Vallabhendra nudging the cat repeatedly with his foot.

The tiger lifted his head.

'Vallabhendra will you stop winding the bloody cat up.' snapped George.

'Wind him up George, wind him up, he doesn't get wound up, does he, *does he*?' taunted Vallabhendra nudging the cat harder and harder. The tiger turned its head and roared. Jayadev pulled his legs up on the seat.

'Who you growling at, you think I'm scared of a grumpy cat?'

Suddenly the tiger got up, growled and snarled its teeth at Vallabhendra.

'*What*?' said Vallabhendra stamping his feet, pretending he was going to charge it. The great tiger let out a blood curdling roar, without warning it charged and leapt at Vallabhendra. Vallabhendra was expecting it and as it brought him down with its immense power he grabbed the cat and swung it round, the pair rolled around on the floor, Vallabhendra got it in a head lock briefly, '*see look who's tough now*?' he taunted. The tiger broke loose with considerable ease and smacked him across the cheek with its paw, it was so hard the slap was easily heard across the room.

'Ow, you bloody great brute,' he said slapping the tiger's shoulder hard, the tiger pinned him down and put its mouth around his throat.

Jayadev sat there watching in disbelief, he was so astounded that he did not notice George pour him another drink as well as one for himself and Vallabhendra.

Vallabhendra threw the tiger off and rolled on top of it, he then put his mouth around the tiger's neck as best he could, 'you see you're not the only one that can bite.' he taunted.

'*You're like a pair of bloody kids*, Jayadev, you want to know why the bloody thing started eating people, well there is your answer.' said George.

Vallabhendra got off, the tiger got up. Vallabhendra ruffled the tiger's fur around its head and started fussing it, the tiger moved in and nuzzled him.

'What's the matter with George? We're just having a little fun that's all.' said Vallabhendra.

'Yes and giving our guests a coronary while you are at it.'

'Nonsense, Jayadev, you weren't afraid of him were you?' asked Vallabhendra pushing the tigers head away as he said it. The tiger responded by playfully biting his arm again.

'Of course not why would I be afraid, it is only the biggest and most ferocious tiger in living history.'

'I wouldn't go that far.' laughed George.

Vallabhendra got up and sat on the big chair next to George, the tiger sat down in front of them, Jayadev smiled broadly.

'The Three Kings of India, seated right in front of me, I cannot believe I did not bring my camera.'

'Kings of India?' What is this malarkey George, we are not kings, we are not even land owners, this land belongs to India and the tigers who roam it, the rumours that have abounded are such nonsense.'

George passed Vallabhendra his drink then he picked up his own. 'That's why you asked me whether we eat the deer raw isn't it?'

'Yes I am afraid so, the rumours are vast and fanciful, indeed I heard you eat raw meat, some even say that you run like the tigers and leap on the deer yourselves.'

George and Vallabhendra burst out in raucous laughter; Jayadev could not help be enraptured by it, he gave a small chuckle himself.

'I hope you can see most rumours are not true.' said George.

'Yes I can, I would like to say thank you for sharing your story with me and explaining the details of my father's death. It has meant a lot to me and not only given me some 'closure' as you would say but has also a reason to rejoice, for this my family will be eternally grateful.'

'Nonsense, you go too far Jayadev.' said George

'No sahib I don't, for I also see now that you never had a choice. I also want you to know that I fully understand every decision you took.'

'Jayadev I see you are a man as honourable as your father, you are always welcome here.' George turned and looked at Vallabhendra.

'Yes, you are, in fact why don't you stay tonight, we have plenty of room, you will be safe in the guest wing of the hotel. It is very luxurious, we will be having a feast tonight around a huge fire in the courtyard, you can be the guest of honour, of course if you want to go out into the jungle, catch your own meat, bring it back and eat it raw, please do so.'

They all laughed.

'Vallabhendra, I would love to sample your cooking I gratefully accept your invitation.'

'Outstanding Gentleman,' said George 'let us finish our drinks and into the day.'

'Why don't you show him around, I need to make sure everything is arranged for later and the delivery has been taken care of.'

'Ok Vallabhendra, I will come and help you in a while, we need to cut some more wood as well, was thinking we could do it together this afternoon.'

'We can get some of the staff to do it.' Vallabhendra replied.

'It would be quicker to just get it done, I can do it alone if you wish, it's up to you?'

'No, we'll do it together, sounds good.' said Vallabhendra slapping George firmly on the arm and walking out.

A few minutes later George and Jayadev walked out into the courtyard and into the blistering hot sun, the white colonial hotel was too bright to look at, they rubbed their eyes to get accustomed to the light. They started to stroll across the huge courtyard.

'You would be surprised at the amount of people who want to live here.'

'Want to live here George, are you serious?'

'What is the one thing you do not have to fear if you live here?'

'I have no idea ... Intruders, I suppose.'

'Think more literal old chap.'

Jayadev stopped and looked around, George could not help but laugh.

'Tigers?' said George.

'Of course, once you are accepted you do not have to fear *tigers*.'

'That is correct Jayadev. I get many letters from people who live in tiger lands and want to come and live here.'

'It is curious but you would be amazed at how many people wish the tiger no harm, even though they live in peril from them.'

'This is not a surprise to me.' replied George.

'Oh ...'

'I have had many requests from people who just want to meet one without being eaten.'

'And that is not a surprise to *me*.'

The two men looked at each other and shared a brief chuckle.

'So what do you think of the place?'

'The place is magnificent, I do not know exactly what I expected. All these tigers milling about the place is simply breathtaking.'

Just as Jayadev said it a tiger walked straight in front of them, George had to stop himself from tripping over it.

'Get out the way you stupid bloody cat,' George said shoving its back hip slightly with his hand, the tiger glanced back at him and walked on. 'I tell you Jayadev they can be a right pain – oh and forget ever having a meal in peace. We often have to time our meals to coincide with theirs in order to be left alone. As with domesticated animals the same is true with these, as soon as they've finished theirs they are in front of yours.'

Jayadev laughed.

'Tell me, how do you run the place, I mean from a financial perspective?'

'My wealth is not needed as many people give generously, we could charge what we want and still fill the hotel any day of the year. We are cautious in choosing our guests to ensure the kingdom's survival, if we opened up to all and sundry the tigers would be driven out or there would be attacks. You see Jayadev I walk you through this courtyard on purpose, all these tigers you see roaming, playing, relaxing, there is one thing about you that they now all know.'

'What is that?'

'That you're with me.'

'I see so I am safe then?'

'I will tell you the same as I do every other visitor, we cannot and do not guarantee your safety. If you do what we tell you to do, you will be fine. It is primarily common sense, do not provoke them, do not walk past them with raw meat.

Do not be fooled these tigers are wild, it is just that we have an understanding, through my tiger, the king as you call him; they have learnt to trust us.'

'It seems strange to me George, yet I am already getting used to them strolling about.'

'It is most peculiar the things that a man can get used to seeing.' said George pulling out a handkerchief and wiping his brow.

'We also sell the tiger's manure to local farmers as it makes an excellent fertilizer; the local farmers said it has increased their crop tenfold.'

'How do you collect it?'

'Well that is the thing I tried to train the tigers all to go in one place but as they are normally territorial it was asking too much. We employ someone to go around and collect it for us. The enterprise is not entirely for fiscal purposes, there are so many big cats here that we would be inundated in fecal matter if we did not sell it incredibly cheap. If a farmer is struggling we'll give it away free or double the amount for the same price.'

'That is a good idea George.'

'Yes, shame it wasn't mine old sport, no, that adulation belongs to Vallabhendra. The huge logs that are standing about are mine though.'

'What are they for, the cats have shredded them.'

'Precisely, we wouldn't have trees left to surround the place otherwise; we are trying to reserve what's natural and keep the balance right. You see that really thin one there.'

'You mean that tiny thin log.'

George laughed, 'that was once a mighty log, it seems to be a particular favourite of the tigers, as you can see they have nearly stripped it down to a candle wick. They are planted right into the ground, some inevitably fall over we leave some of them laying on the ground to give the cats a bit of variety.'

'We all like a bit of variety.'

'Yes, I suppose we do Jayadev.'

They strolled through the open space to the hotel where they were greeted by a small Indian man with a long pony tail that ran down his back, he also had a thin groomed moustache.

'Jayadev, this is Palak.'

'Nice to meet you, what do you do here?'

'I manage the tigers in the hotel and see that only those who are supposed to be in here overnight are, I also make sure none of them become a nuisance.'

'And he does a fine Job too.'

'Thank you George.' said Palak, making way for them to enter the hotel.

'So how many staff do you have here George?'

'About fifteen, we try to employ only people of strong character, as animals have a way of detecting fear and it could cause an attack.'

'I see you and Vallabhendra have been rigorous in your responsibilities.'

'We have a unique opportunity here, only a fool would flounder it.'

They walked through the great parlour that was decked with marble pillars. Jayadev stopped to marvel at all the fancy furnishings that had somehow remained unblemished even though the tigers regularly pass through the room.

George showed him the infirmary where sick and old tigers were being cared for, Jayadev was introduced to the two vets and the assistant, who being a rather large man, was there to help to keep the tigers under control.

They viewed the other side of the hotel that was off limits to all felines, except The Great Tiger King. The doors were solid and locked fast. In this wing was the plush restaurant and the same bar that Charles, Robert, Gerald and Alastair had all drank in with George previously. There was also another grand looking parlour.

George personally escorted Jayadev up the stairs and stopped outside a double set of wooden white painted doors with gold handles on.

'Jayadev, this will be your room while you stay with us. Please make yourself at home, you can come and go as you please but I would request certainly for the first day or two that you do not leave the hotel wing without an escort. It's nothing to worry about but it does not harm to err on the side of caution.'

'May I?' asked Jayadev gesturing toward the door handle.

'Be my guest.' said George with a warm smile.

Jayadev pushed open the door and walked into a large room. There was a huge four poster bed complete with mosquito net, a writing desk and chair, two armchairs and a coffee table, a small sideboard with an array of decanters and refreshments on it and several small bookshelves adorned with a variety of books.

'Really George, this is too much all I need is a bed.'

'Nonsense you are our guest and you shall be treated as such. If you look through this door you will see that you also have a private bathroom.'

Jayadev, walked into the marble bathroom, there was a large bath with gold finishing's.

'I must warn you George, you may have a difficult time asking me to leave if you carry on like this.'

'There is a cord by your bed, pull it if you need anything. A bell will ring and a member of staff will come to your assistance, you are welcome to order food or drinks to your room, it is all free as is the bar and restaurant downstairs.'

'Your generosity knows no bounds, I will honour this generosity.'

'No need, there is one more thing however, I would like to give you this.' said George pulling out a silver whistle and handing it over, 'it is a policeman's whistle all the way from England, you are to keep it on you at all times, if for whatever reason you find yourself in danger from a tiger or it is a real emergency blow it as hard as you can. Everybody is required to carry one at all times.'

Jayadev examined it carefully, 'my father told me about these once, your policeman that they have a strange name if I recall.'

'They are known as Bobbies.'

'Ah yes, that was it.'

'I have some work to be getting on with so if you do not mind I will leave you to yourself for a while. I will have your bags brought up to you shortly. We have decided to have a feast tonight in your honour. Normally we entertain guests in the restaurant. Some years back myself and Vallabhendra hit upon the idea of feasting like a tribe every once in a while. We light a huge fire, roll some logs round it to use as seating and then feast on tiger provided deer. We cook the meat over the huge roaring fire, then drink and chat into the night, does that sound acceptable to you? Vallabhendra seems to think you might enjoy it.'

'Yes, thank you, again I would be most honoured.'

'Excellent, I will meet you about seven at the bar, we will have an evening drink before we head out.'

'Sounds grand, I will have a sleep I think, I am not used to drink during the day.' said Jayadev looking slightly unsteady on his feet.

George gave a short laugh and closed the door behind him.

~

The axe heads glistened like huge diamonds in the bright sun. The two mighty men with large ripped muscles brought the heads smashing into the giant logs, sweat poured from them yet neither man stopped. As if there were machine they chopped and chopped.

'That ought to do it.' said Vallabhendra.

'I would have thought so we have enough to last us a week let alone a night. Let's go and wash up.'

'Yes, good idea.'

'I told Jayadev we will pick him up from the bar about seven.'

'Would you mind getting him George, I would like to prepare the meat whoever did it last time didn't do the best of jobs, I had enough fur in my mouth by the end of the meal to make a coat.'

'Well it wasn't me old chap. I will ask Palak to collect him.'

'Yes, that is a good idea.'

~

Seven o'clock came around. The heat of the day had passed, tigers that had been sheltering from the heat began to stir.

Men busied themselves carrying chopped logs and placing them in the middle of the enclosure. There was an area of scorched earth where the fire was always held. Vallabhendra and George carried over some huge logs one at a time and placed them strategically around the fire to form seating.

After they had washed and put on fresh clothes, George and Vallabhendra returned to the fireplace where they found Palak and Jayadev sitting on a log by the unlit fire. Tigers were walking about everywhere.

'There is a huge army base not far from here you know.' said Palak.

'Yes I do know actually, I paid it a visit as soon as I got off the train.' replied Jayadev.

'Evening Jayadev I trust you enjoyed your afternoon.' said George interrupting their conversation.

'Immensely George, I slept for nearly all of it, did some scribing in my journal, had a cup of tea then came to see you.'

'You were offered a drink down at the bar before you came I hope.'

'Yes, I refused the offer as I fear there will be consumption tonight and I have not the tolerance that you all seem to possess I am afraid.'

'Ha.' Vallabhendra laughed and slapped George on the back. 'He knows you too well, and that Jayadev is something to be proud of.'

'You drink just as much me you fiend, it was *me* that stopped *you* the other night as I recall.' said George.

'You're both as bad as each other.' said Palak swishing his braided pony tail behind his back.

'*Use some fuel Zubhasamanvit, for crying out loud we will be here until Christmas the way you're going on.*' shouted George to an Indian man in a blue t-shirt who was attempting unsuccessfully to light the fire.

The man sauntered off and returned with a can of fuel. George took it off him and poured it over the chopped logs and straw.

'*Everybody back, come on off your seats and move back the lot of you.*' shouted George. They all got off the logs and stepped back. 'Vallabhendra, give me a hand with the cats will you.'

George and Vallabhendra began clapping their hands loudly and shooing away the tigers, '*Come on be off with you.*' they shouted.

'What are they doing?' asked Jayadev.

'They are shooing off the cats because they are using a large amount of fuel to ignite the fire, when they light it there will be a mighty flame that will singe anyone in the vicinity and also startle the cats. The tigers trust Vallabhendra and George implicitly, without them I doubt there would be one man on this earth with the courage to try and run this place.'

'Interesting.' said Jayadev.

The sky lit up orange and yellow as George set the fire alight. Jayadev was indeed glad he had moved back as the flame was enormous. Some of the tigers roared in apparent protestation but soon simmered down.

They all took their places around the fire, after a few minutes other people joined them. Muttering, laughing and tumultuous greetings were all that could be heard above the roaring flames.

People's faces glowed in the roaring campfire. George and Vallabhendra bought a huge structure over, it looked like a tent frame but it had a full grown deer tied to it by its feet. The deer had been meticulously skinned.

They placed the frame over the fire. It wasn't long before the smell of cooking meat filled the air. The whisky and beer bottles started flowing around the fire. When the body had cooked to perfection the legs were hacked off to finish cooking on their own. Huge piles of freshly cooked meat were slung on plates. George and Vallabhendra had huge portions, Vallabhendra practically ate a whole leg to himself. There was bread, potato, chickpea, vegetable mix and other assortments but it was mostly untouched by George, Vallabhendra and Palak who tucked into the venison like a pack of carnivorous dinosaurs.

'Where is the great tiger king?' asked Jayadev.

George and Vallabhendra laughed.

'Look behind you.' said George.

Jayadev looked over his shoulder and saw the tiger sitting up right behind them with his glittering coat of fire. He moved back in fright, the tiger looking as giant as ever was watching the men drooling intently.

'Oh yes, I am sure you are sitting there for the company aren't you just so lonely you couldn't stay away.'

The great cat twitched his head as it tried to work out George's comments.

'Oh cos you don't want anything else do you.' said George lobbing a huge slab of cooked meat at it, the tiger immediately sprang forth, caught it with its teeth and almost ate it in one.

'You're supposed to taste it you stupid cat.' continued George.

Vallabhendra motioned for the guy in charge of the meat for a big piece. Vallabhendra put it firmly in his mouth, got up and leaning in with his hands on the big log put his head down towards the tiger and started growling.

The tiger hunched down as if stalking and crept towards Vallabhendra's face, then it too started growling. Jayadev watched astounded, George and Palak sat there grinning.

The tiger grabbed the meat gently, as soon as it did Vallabhendra pulled it away again. The tiger growled and pulled the meat back. Vallabhendra went with it, but he pulled back and the tiger yanked at it again. Vallabhendra started to pull back when the tiger lost its patience and ripped it out of Vallabhendra's mouth as if he had been holding it with his lips.

'*Be patient you stupid cat, you nearly ripped my bloody teeth out.*'

There was a cacophony of laughter around the campfire.

Ten minutes later Vallabhendra tapped Jayadev on the shoulder, 'Look behind you now.'

Jayadev looked behind him and realised they were completely surrounded by tigers. The cats were all sitting in a circle as if it was some kind of ritual. Jayadev looked across the fire; behind the people sitting on the logs across from him great orange cats flickered in the background all sitting in a perfect circle around the camp.

'We are surrounded.' said Jayadev gulping.

Vallabhendra laughed his mighty laugh. 'I thought that might test your nerves.'

'*Stop winding him up.*' snapped George.

'It is such fun, I apologise Jayadev, here have a drink you look like you need one, Jayadev took the bottle and had a large swig.'

'I am not an easy man to spook but my heart palpitates as we speak.'

'There is no need, they are just after meat, that is why we are cooking extra.'

'I wondered why you were cooking more deer, I thought we can't possibly eat more.'

'Come on Vallabhendra let's sort these cats out.' said George.

They got up and started clapping and shouting, the tigers moved off and followed them as they walked to the other side of the fire, they took the two huge cooked deer and sliced chunks off until there was a huge pile of cooked meat then they walked away from the fire and started throwing chunks of cooked venison to the tigers. The Great Tiger King stayed exactly where he was, he was now laying down behind the log where they were all seated. Palak saw him looking.

'He does what he want.' said Palak.

After all the meat had been distributed, George and Vallabhendra ran at the tigers shouting and waving their arms. They were greeted by angry roars and growls, but it did not faze them, they chased the tigers away.

George and Vallabhendra returned to their seats. George was carrying a huge piece of cooked venison which he threw to the Great Tiger King, it leapt up and caught it before the meat could touch the ground.

George poured some more whisky and passed the bottle round, every one filled their glasses, an ice bucket was also passed around.

'You know Vallabhendra the thing that surprised me the most about this place is all the logistics that goes into running it.'

'Elaborate my friend, what do you mean?'

'Like the giant scratching posts, the manure, thinking of the cats before you lit the fire - that would have never occurred to me.'

'Yes I see what you mean. Most of it came through trial and error, if it wasn't for George's uncanny ability with them we would have been gobbled up years ago. Of course I am now becoming as familiar with them as he is but it has taken many years.'

'You were employed by him at one point were you not?'

'Yes, he was good to me. He is the first white man I met that treated me as his equal. We are close friends now, more like brothers, nothing will ever come between us.'

As he said that the great tiger king crept up behind Vallabhendra and George and nuzzled his giant head between them.

'What do you want, you great oaf.' said George as the tiger forced its way between them both, laying over the log it began to purr. Both the men started stroking and needling the tiger's giant head with their nearest hand, the cat purred louder.'

'You were saying Vallabhendra.' said Jayadev.

'Apart from him of course.' Vallabhendra replied.

'I told you Jayadev, he's like a bloody big kid.' said George.

The group drank the night away, as their talk and laughter gave way to not much more than inebriated mumblings they fell asleep one by one until eventually the crimson sun arose and the jungle stirred in the morning mist. The tigers had started going to bed after a night of their own frivolity or so it seemed. Whenever George and Vallabhendra threw one of their deer cooking parties the tigers would always be particularly hyper, chasing each other through the jungle and generally larking about.

The men stirred about dawn as the sun was rising, the tiger king awoke George and Vallabhendra, they headed inside, in the sudden comfort of their own beds they slept until lunchtime. Jayadev and Palak did the same.

It was gone noon when people started to rise again. George got up and washed himself, he sat with a cup of tea inside his palatial tent and contemplated the day ahead. After he had finished his tea, he cleared the morning cobwebs out of his mind and went outside. Some of the other men had already started clearing up, the tigers were mostly sleeping in the shade.

He started clearing the bottles and leftover plates, then he turned his attention to the fire, it all needed to be cleared. He threw water all over the ashes and started moving the partially and unburnt wood to the fire pile for next time. Looking up he saw Jayadev and Palak walking across the courtyard.

'Nary have I had a night like that George, thank you I had a time I can tell you but never has a head hurt like this.' said Jayadev.

George laughed and slapped the top of Jayadev's arm. 'You'll be alright old boy.'

'Would you like a hand?'

'Why not Jayadev, if you feel up to it.'

'If it is ok George I will be getting back to the hotel.' said Palak.

'Yes that is fine, thank you for your help. Do not forget we have visitors arriving in a few days.'

'Very good George I will ensure we are prepared.'

Palak turned and walked off across the courtyard.

'We need to take these logs behind that small barn looking building.' said George

They picked up some of the largish logs and carried them over to the barn, they walked behind it and threw them on the log pile. They returned to the fire.

'Not much left just move these and give the yard a bit of a brush, the men are doing the rest.' said George.

Jayadev looked across the yard and saw two men re-erecting one of the scratching posts. George mopped his brow with his forearm.

'Something is not right.'

'What do you mean George?' Jayadev replied.

George stood there staring down the drive way.

'George are you alright, what is the matter?'

'Look at the trees.'

Jayadev looked and saw the treetops swaying.

'So?'

'So? It is not windy my dear boy.'

'Apologies George, you have me at a loss.'

'If the wind is not moving the trees, then what is old man?'

'Tigers.' replied Jayadev.

George broke his gaze and gave jayadev an incredulous look.

'Don't be a fool, only monkeys move treetops like that. And as they are used to the tigers there must be something at odds, a tiger rampaging or something.

The movement of treetops started to move closer as if the trees were doing a Mexican wave.

They heard the monkeys call. Jayadev felt himself gulp.

George stood there with his hands on his hips waiting, a faint rumbling came from the distance. Tigers began to roar, the thunder got closer and closer as if the world was speaking. The tigers in the yard awoke, they jumped to their feet and began to roar. The sky turned dark, filled with birds and bats, anything that was not tiger fled the area.

George stood there un-phased with his hands still on his hips waiting. Jayadev stepped closer. The men working in the yard all stopped and looked at George.

The sound was tremendous.

'Then George saw a huge tiger running up the middle of the road, there was something odd about it, it seemed somehow deformed, the shape at the front didn't seem right, he could not quite believe what he was seeing.

The Great Tiger King ran up to George and sat next to him, George patted his head gently several times while watching the other tiger approaching from the road.

Finally it entered the courtyard and what he thought he saw made sense. Jayadev gasped as the tiger ran straight up to George and dropped a huge decapitated Tigers head at his feet.

'*Good God.*' said George.

'Why has it killed another tiger and chewed its head off?'

'It hasn't.' said George leaning down and rolling the head over to examine it, 'this head has been hacked off with a machete and one thing do I know is that tiger's do not use machete's.'

The tiger's all took an attack stance, the roars were so loud it was unbearable.

'*Silence!*' George yelled as loud as he could, waving his hands sharply. All the tigers stopped, after a few seconds the whole jungle fell quiet.

'Look.' said Jayadev. 'There is another tiger coming down the road. It looks like he carrying a ball.'

'That's no ball.' said George.

The tiger was running full speed when it ran straight into the courtyard. The great cat dropped a man's head at George's feet.

'*Good God* indeed George, what is going on, that is the head of a white man he must be army.'

'No, look how scruffily unshaven he is, that is not the army.'

'Some unfortunate visitor or poacher who thought he could sneak in?'

'In normal circumstances I would agree but someone deliberately hacked off that tigers head, that was an act of war I can tell it in my gut. No, whoever would be brave enough to enter this kingdom to create havoc must be both very courageous and very well paid – I would imagine they are mercenaries.'

'But why?'

'That is the riddle Jayadev. I have fought on many a battlefield and in many an ambush as a result, I have developed an instinct for this type of thing, I can tell you more trouble is coming and in a big way. I want you to leave immediately, there is a back trail I will send an escort of tigers with you and some men. You should be safe.'

'No George, my father stood his test of honour, it is obvious that fate has now linked my family to you, we shall go down in history proud. Even though I am scared I shall stand by you and your tigers.'

'I will let you into a secret, in war everybody is scared, it is only about how you handle it.'

The tigers were all looking at George, The Great Tiger King paced about growling deeply.

Palak came running across the courtyard.

'What is going on?'

'*Men, come quickly.*' shouted George.

The two men who had been erecting the posts came over, several more came running out of the barns to join them. Other men came running out of various places until there was a small crowd gathered round staring in astonishment at the two bloody heads on the floor.

'*Where the bloody hell is Vallabhendra?*' George yelled.

The men shrugged their shoulders, there was no answer.

'Something is happening, I don't know what but it looks like we might be under attack. Palak, alert all staff at the hotel, then get out of here as soon as you can and alert the governor and the army that we are in trouble. I am sure they have nothing to do this.'

'How can you be so sure?' asked one of the men.

'Because that's not cricket and that's not how we do things. I don't know why but there must be a private army behind this as I doubt anyone other than a raving lunatic would try and cause trouble in these lands on their own.

Anyone who wants to go please do so now. Palak is going to notify the authorities so I suggest you go with him, some tigers will accompany you as well.'

'George I will do as you ask, then I shall return to be by your side.' said Palak adjusting his boots to make them tight.

'Stay out of harm's way my friend, I suggest you all go, this is my fight.'

'Nonsense, we are as much a part of this kingdom as you are, these cats mean as much to us as they do to you.' said the man that Jayadev had seen the night before trying to light the fire.

'Apologies Zubhasamanvit, you are quite right. We will stand together and see what happens. But we must expect trouble.'

'My Tigers, my cats, my children, come, those who are near.' The Great Tiger King gave a fearsome roar, tigers appeared from everywhere and surrounded them.

George held up the man's decapitated head, he looked at the tigers and then at the Great Tiger King, he looked serious, a flash of rage crossed his crimson face. George nodded at the great tiger king, pointed at the head and then flicked his arm toward the jungle.

The tigers dispersed in every direction, roaring past they leapt into different parts of the jungle. The great tiger king remained at George's side. George flicked his head toward the jungle and the tiger king ran, his great powerful muscles flexing as the great cat went looking to avenge once again.

'War has been declared.' said George throwing his head back to the dirt. Men prepare yourselves, you know where the guns are, arm yourselves, if any man comes out of the jungle - unless he has his arms clearly in the air or is waving a white flag - you fire on them.'

They heard the blood curdling scream of a man being killed by a tiger.

'They, whoever they are, are getting close. We will arm ourselves and set up a defensive perimeter. We must act fast, pass my message onto any other staff you see, flee or fight I care not but you must to decide now. We will meet back here in five minutes. Jayadev, go with them it will be safer for you, if you're staying arm yourself, the others will provide guns for you.'

'I will arm myself and fight alongside you George.' Jayadev replied with a determined look in his face.

The men nodded their heads at George and wandered off toward the hotel. George set off for his tent, he was thinking of what was afoot. What could possibly be happening? It would not be the British Army, especially with his war record, he was still hailed as a hero. His thoughts turned to Vallabhendra, he cursed to himself that if anything happened to Vallabhendra he would avenge him no matter what. George calmed himself, he knew to get angry could affect his logic, he might miss something vital.

'Ha, I never thought it would be *this* easy, don't you move sir.'

George startled, turned to see a man in dressed in black aiming a gun at him.

'*Who the hell do think you are pointing a gun at me, you think I am scared of a bullet?*' said George walking toward him.

'I was warned you were tough, don't test me.' the man said.

'George stopped, slyly watched his beloved tiger creeping up behind the man.'

'You're a merc, you're certainly not British, not German either, you are European though.'

'Good with accents too I see, shut your mouth.'

'Let me go now and I promise you shall live.'

'You stupid fool, your war record doesn't scare me.'

George relaxed, the man upon seeing this grew concerned. He was watching his hands closely, but George was unarmed.

'*My* war record may not concern you, but I think his should.' said George pointing behind his assailant.

The man turned around and saw the huge tiger behind him, the man dropped his gun, his eyes opened wide with fright, before he could gasp the tiger leapt and literally tore him apart.

A man stepped out carrying a rifle, George instantly recognised it as a .505 *Gibbs*. He aimed it straight at the tiger. George was about to plead with him, when there was a loud crack as the man's neck snapped like a twig, he dropped to the floor as if he had no skeleton, standing behind him was Vallabhendra.

'*Where the bloody hell have you been?*' snapped George.

'I was out in the jungle when I heard the commotion, it took me a while to get back, what's going on?'

'I'm not sure, we seem to be under attack they decapitated one of our tigers, but another tiger brought one of *their* head's back, so we're even on that front. From what I can deduce someone has hired a mercenary force and engaged it against us. I knew it wouldn't be the army, they would consult with us first for one thing.'

'I am going to get my weapons.'

'I have told the staff to flee, they wouldn't have it so I ordered them to arm themselves then meet me in the courtyard. After I get my guns, I will be out there.'

'I won't be long, I told you we should have kept that fence high.'

'*Yes, alright Valla, I get your bloody point.*' Vallabhendra laughed and walked off.

George ran inside and grabbed his army issue *Webley* revolver along with the holster. As he was doing so he spotted the Indian army uniform with its sandy coloured top and sandy green bottoms that Vallabhendra had given him as a present. He put it on, grabbed his rifle, filled his webbing with ammo, grabbed his canteen and filled it with water, then he put some military issue dry snacks in some of the webbing. Albeit he had long left the army, the lifestyle he led in India let him keep in touch with a lot of practices that once back home in England you would quickly forget.

George ran out into the courtyard and saw that some of the men had already returned. He ran over to them.

'Myself and Valla have just had a run in with two men, both are dead and both were mercenaries.'

The men all looked at each other.

'I am hoping these two tried to do the job alone. I am not sure what they wanted but they were interested in *me*, it makes sense as myself and Valla run the compound. However I still cannot be sure of their motives. Until we are I want you to stay within the compound. You cannot be held responsible for defending your home.'

Valla came running toward them he was dressed in dark green with a black turban, a shiny golden dagger inserted in the front of it. The dagger at his side now resembled a small sword, he had a revolver and rifle also.

'Good you are here, I was just saying it would be a good idea to defend the perimeter.' said George.

'Yes excellent idea, George we are all with you, you needn't worry about that.'

'Ha Vallabhendra, have you ever known me to be worried about *anything*.'

'That is true my friend, sometimes I think you do not worry enough. You have that glint in your eye again, you are seeking mischief I can tell.'

'I assure you anyone who comes after my cats, I shall come after them.' said George emphatically.

The men all cheered.

'Sir, Palak has set off to do as you ask, but he told me to tell you he will return immediately regardless of what you say.'

'That sounds like Palak alright.' said George. 'He always was a good sport.'

'There are only twelve of us if you include me and George, thirteen when Palak returns but we will defend our homes, our lives and our beloved tigers with honour.' said Valla pulling out his long dagger and holding it in the air.

The men all cheered.

'We have plenty of ammo but we don't know how many there are, so only fire when absolutely necessary and make your shot count, remember this is not a military base.

Four men either side of the oval and two at each end. What do you think Valla?' said George staring deep into the Jungle.

'I am wondering whether we should go out and meet them.' replied Vallabhendra.

'The tigers will defend us.' added George.

As they said that a volley of frantic shots rang out followed by a man's scream.

'That's another one gone.' said one of the men.

A tiger ran across the road but was brought down in a hail of bullets, bullets then started coming at the men.

'George the posts quick.' shouted Valla.

The two men with their immense strength pushed two erected mighty tree logs over that had been used as scratching posts. The huge logs crashed to the ground.

The men realising why they were doing it dived behind the trunks and opened fire.

'Cover us.' said George.

George and Valla ran through a wall of bullets towards the road and the fallen tiger. Bullets danced all around them as they ran to a wood pile and slid behind it.

Both men checked their weapons.

'On three, ready Valla?'

'Yes.'

'Good. Three.' said George standing up and opening fire in the direction of where the gunfire had come from. Fire was returned from the jungle, one bullet hit the top of the wood pile.

'Cover me Valla, I think there is something we have missed.' said George.

'Ok, go my friend.' said Valla slapping him on the back.

George got up and ran across the single opening in the sawn log fence. He dived behind some logs. Immediately he checked over the log fence as the logs was to his side and only knee height. George saw a large tiger laying in a bush, he motioned for it to stay where it was. He looked back at the road, anger filled his eyes when he saw the tiger laying there dead.

He rolled back, brazenly stood up then ducked back down again. As he did a bullet hit the ground just in front of him, just as he thought. He leant around the logs, looked at Valla and signalled to stand up on the count of three and fire into the jungle in front of him.

Valla nodded to George his understanding. George counted aloud using his fingers and upon showing the third Vallabhendra stood up and started firing, within seconds George stood up and made a perfect shot straight into the sniper that had been hiding in the tree. When Valla had started firing the sniper had turned his attention to picking him off, a mistake that he would not live to regret.

George signalled to Valla again who was reloading, on the count of three the men got up simultaneously. As soon as they did George whistled to the tiger in the bush, the tiger ran across the road as they fired a volley of shots.

The man stood up not knowing who to aim at, he panicked and took aim at the charging tiger, George put him down with his *Webley*, the man thudded to the ground with a hole in his chest, seconds later his throat was ripped out.

'They're certainly adventurous folk, aren't they Valla?'

'So are we George, so are we.' said Vallabhendra with a laugh.

The jungle fell silent.

'It is too quiet, what do you think they are doing Valla?'

'Hard to tell, if they have the man power and are being cautious they could be testing our perimeter.'

'Excellent thinking Valla, let's pull back.'

George whistled and four or five tigers came out of hiding, he motioned and they all ran off into the jungle and climbed into trees.

'Where's our tiger?' said Valla.

'I don't know, we cannot worry about him, you know what he's like, he'll turn up when you need him.'

The two men ran back into the courtyard, grabbed one the logs and separated it, so they had cover from both sides.

'*They are testing our perimeter be on the lookout they could come from any direction.*' shouted George.

The men set their guns up to cover either angle.

'We are not spread out enough George.'

'I know Vallabhendra, I know ...' the oval rang out with shots, all the men took cover, as fire came in from the opposite side as predicted.

'I have to go there is something I forgot.'

Under a hail of bullets George ran as fast as he could back to the tent. He arrived just in time to discover a mercenary sneaking in through the back. George lifted his revolver and before the man could realise he was shot in the head, he fell with the gun still in his hand.

George walked over, took the gun, then cautiously went through the back of the tent, there was no one else. He thought it odd that there should be just one on his own.

George ran to a huge chest that was locked tight, he pulled out his keys and unlocked it. At the bottom of the trunk was a box of grenades, he pulled them out of the boxes and put them in a large military canvas bag. There were also some German ones that he had acquired, he put those in too. Throwing the bag over his shoulder more violently than anticipated he left the room, as he did he knew he had just made a vital mistake. A soldiers instinct told him that a gun was trained on him, they had let him think he was alone so they could get an easy shot, the oldest trick in the book and he had fallen for it. 'Damn it!' George cursed to himself.

Without a sound George, took his finger off the trigger and carefully maneuvered the gun so he was holding the butt between his index finger and thumb. There was no way he was going to drop or throw it without being instructed to. He half expected to be shot there and then, after all the man with the gun must be standing over the dead body of someone on his team.

He turned slowly to face the man, his gun held up so he could see it. The man had yellow straw hair, a moustache and several days' worth of unshaven stubble.

'What do you bloody lunatics want?' George demanded.

The man lifted his gun as if to be sure not to miss, he opened his mouth, as he did so there was an orange flash. The perpetrator lowered his weapon, his mouth dropped open as if a hinge had broken on his jaw, he looked down watching his own intestines spilling out of him, hitting the floor like sausages. Organs made angry splats as they landed. The man looked up at George and fell to the floor dead.

'Thanks but you could have waited a second.' said George with a face twixt of both anger and happiness.

The great tiger king ignored his remark. George heard several dull thuds, then another, then two more. Out of the corner of his eye he glimpsed a blackish silver oval shape land on the ground.

'*Run!*' screamed George to his beloved tiger. They ran out of the marquee as fast they could. George was suddenly blown off his feet, he went flying face forward into the dirt. The marquee was completely gone, bits of shrapnel and fabric rained down.

'So they have Grenades too.' said George, nervously checking the bag of grenades on his back, all seemed to be in order. The tiger was ok, George got up and immediately started firing into the smoke. Expecting a charge, Valla and some of the men came running firing their guns, George ran across to them.

'*To the jungle, it's our only hope.*' George yelled. Valla whistled to the other men.

'Come on Vallabhendra, let's go near the road.' said George.

'Are you mad that's where the fighting began.'

'Just trust me Valla ...' There was a huge explosion, one of the barns went up in flames.'

'That was explosives.' said George.

'Are you sure it wasn't a well placed Grenade.'

'No it bloody wasn't Valla.'

'What about the Hotel, we could use that?' said one of the men with a jet black beard and rolled up cloth tied around his head.

'We would just be trapping ourselves.' said George.

'Agreed,' said Valla 'but are we sure it has been cleared?'

'I don't know are we?' the bearded man asked.

The men all looked at each other.

'Me and the cat are going to check the hotel, set up a perimeter just inside the jungle where I shot the man out of the tree, go, now, I will meet you there as soon as I can.'

'*You're not bloody going alone George I can tell you.*' snapped Vallabhendra.

The two men ran toward the hotel, the giant tiger ran alongside them at the same speed, just a trot to him but full pace for the Valla and George. They heard a single shot ring out, they stopped and looked back just in time to see one of the men fall with a bullet in his back, the others kept running. There was a huge explosion that sent Vallabhendra and George to the ground. It was so large that the ground shook.

They looked up at the hotel, the whole thing was engulfed in flames, one of the wings collapsed.

'They blew the hotel up, I mean the whole bloody thing, George.' said Valla.

'Damn the confounded bastards they must have been in there while we have been busy fighting.' replied George.

'I hope nobody was in there, if there was they'd be dead, at least we know Palak got out.' said Vallabhendra.

'Yes, you are right, come on Vallabhendra there is nothing we can do let's get back to the others.'

The pair of them retreated cautiously George drew his rife for a long shot, they crept back across the courtyard without incident and were soon regrouped with the others. The men were all praying for their deceased friend, who was still laying in the courtyard with a hole in his back.

'Gentlemen, this is no time for prayer we will lament Qutuz later and do what is right by him I assure you. For now though we must decide what we are going to do.' George stepped closer to Jayadev, 'Are you ok?'

'Yes I am fine George, before I will admit I was somewhat frightened which is why I have been so silent, but now I am angry ... to shoot a man in the back like that. Have these men any courage, any honour?'

'That's right Jayadev, how dare they be so discourteous?' said Valla.

'Let's decide what we are going to do, we should be safe here for a couple of minutes.' repeated George.

'I fear we are not safe anywhere.' said one the men who was wearing an inappropriate yellow shirt.

'Let us not waste time arguing, what are you thinking George?' asked Jayadev.

'I am thinking that we are being toyed with. Do not ask me why or by whom, there is something odd about this whole situation.'

The Great Tiger King suddenly bolted away into the dense jungle on the other side of the road.

'Where is he off to?'

'Don't know George, we can't go after him, we just have to trust he knows what he is doing.' Vallabhendra replied.

They heard a man scream way off in the jungle.

'Yes, I think he knows.' said jayadev. The group of men all had a small laugh at this.

'Why didn't they attack, I would have destroyed all the buildings simultaneously and moved in for the kill, they obviously had us surrounded.' said George rubbing his chin.

'The tigers must have helped.' said the man in the yellow shirt.

'They did and they are not finished yet as you just heard.' said Valla.

'For some reason they are playing a game, I will elaborate. When they shot Qutuz why didn't they shoot anyone else? They had plenty of time and plenty of chance. No, they are waiting for something or they're taunting us. Their overall intentions are now clear. This is no skirmish, to destroy the whole hotel like that, be under no illusion we are at war, I think myself and Vallabhendra and I imagine our cat are still their primary target. I intend to strike first.'

'Where will they strike from?' asked Jayadev.

'It is unlikely that it will be the road, it is way too obvious and if the army or anyone else were to come to our aid this would be the route that they would take.'

'Exactly Vallabhendra. They are coming through the dense jungle, this has been meticulously planned, the timing is no coincidence. We have no guests and a skeleton staff running at the moment. With distinguished guests arriving next week the staff will be tripled, even quadrupled, and some them will bring their own security. No one knew of Jayadev's arrival even if they did it would be of little consequence, he is just one man travelling alone. No offence Jayadev.'

'None taken.' said Jayadev hanging on George's every word.

There was a scuffling noise in the trees, they all turned and looked up in a nearby tree, a large tiger had moved. It had adjusted its poise to strike, suddenly it leapt through the air with claws and fangs out.

'*No*,' yelled George. '*No. We want him alive, no, I said no, we want him alive.*'

George was running, pushing his way through the jungle, everybody followed, it was only a minute or two before they came across them.

The tiger seemed to have listened to George, it's claws were deeply embedded into the man's gun arm, he had dropped his weapon. Blood was running everywhere, the tiger had clawed his legs and arms and had his mouth poised at his throat.

'Good boy,' said George ruffling the tigers head as if it were a dog having retrieved a pheasant.

'Come on leave him.' said Valla pushing the cat off the fallen assassin.

'*I surrender, I surrender, please do not let the cat eat me, I beg you sir I beg you.*'

'Can you walk?' snapped George.

Valla began searching the man, he removed some Grenades as well as another pistol and the man's rifle. He inspected his wounds.

'Some of these cuts are deep George but I think he'll live.'

'Come on let's take him back to where we were.' said George.

The man winced as he was forced to limp, aided by George and Valla.

When they got back to the little clearing where they had been chatting, Jayadev examined the area a little more closely. 'I see why you wanted us to meet here George, look at all the tigers hiding in the trees. We have the best alarm system you could possibly want.'

'Exactly that is why I asked the tigers to hide in the trees around here. I knew early on that the attack wouldn't be coming from the road, albeit that is precisely what we were supposed to think. It was only logical that they would keep sending some men this way to convince us.'

Vallabhendra got out his water bottle and offered some to the bleeding man who was laying against a tree trunk half in pain, half mesmerised by the amount of tigers hiding in the trees.

'Are you comfortable fiend.' said George sharply. 'I have a proposition for you, if you converse upon us the whole truth as you know it, we will treat you as a prisoner of war. This means you shall be fed, watered and your wounds tended to. If you refuse we shall do everything we can to make you talk and I will have no hesitation in ending your life should I deem it necessary. You will be handed into the authorities, we cannot promise that you will not hang but you will be given a sporting chance, so what is it to be?'

The man winced as he sat upright a little more. He had dirty brown hair and a shallow unkempt beard.

'What do you want to know?'

George sat down so he was on the same level as the man.

'You are a mercenary are you not?'

'Yes.'

'Who hired you?'

'I don't know.'

Valla leant down to grab him but George stopped him. George looked the man straight in his eyes, without looking away he clicked his fingers, the huge tiger that had attacked him came skulking forward to finish its meal.

'*No, no I am not lying I do not know who he is, we do not know who he is, I swear it, I swear as God is my witness sir I do not lie.*'

'Confound it why do you not know who it is?'

'The mercenary business is a shady one but believe it or not there is some kind of structure. We work for ourselves yet there are people who make it their business to find us work. One of the people I use for such purposes reached out to me about a job that pays immensely well. I was informed that I could not know who it was, I would however essentially be working for the British Army.'

'*You bloody what*?' said Valla.

'*It's lies I won't hear of it.*' snapped George grabbing the man around the neck.

'*I swear it.*' The man protested.

'Why should we believe you?' asked Valla leaning down and putting his hands on his knees.

'Because ... because I have proof, *I have proof.*' The man shrieked excitedly. '*In my webbing there is folded up letter, it is a copy handed to us as proof,* it certainly worked as we thought we were acting for a legitimate cause.'

George leant over and opened the pouch that the man had indicated with his head, he opened the piece of paper and read it.

'What does it say?' asked Valla.

'The gist of it is that we have been allowing innocent people to be eaten and feeding local villagers to our tigers ...'

'*But we protect and feed all the local villages.*' shouted Vallabhendra.

'That both the British and Indian authorities are at a loss as what to do as the Indian people revere the tiger and do not want them all killed. In order to bring these terrorists to justice they grant permission for a carefully assembled private army to take over the grounds by any means necessary, once successful they are to hand it over to the British Army.

Utter claptrap, never have I read such an insidious pack of lies, here Vallabhendra have a look for yourself.'

George handed the letter to Vallabhendra who skimmed through it, his face got angrier and angrier.

'Who gave you this letter?' Valla asked through gritted teeth.

'The man in charge.' The man replied obsequiously.

'Who is that?' demanded Vallabhendra.

'He is a Mercenary and is unofficially in charge. I do not know him we all rendezvoused in India and were debriefed by him, then given a copy of this letter in case anyone should question what we are doing.'

'You realise you have been set up?' said George.

'*What do you mean?*' said the man again wincing in pain.

'I mean this letter is fraudulent, it is supposedly signed by General Renhold, that is not his signature.'

'How do you know?' the man asked.

'Because I am close personal friends with the General and have a multitude of letters signed by his hand. Also,' George turned and looked at everyone else. 'you remember I said that we have some important dignitaries visiting next week, well General Renhold is one of them. Furthermore, he alone has been one of our strongest advocates, we would have had to vacate many years ago if it were not for him, so please forgive me sir if I call this letter *a load of bollocks*!' George shouted.

'Most extraordinary.' said Jayadev rubbing his chin.

'*Do you not read the papers man*, the tiger kingdom is famed throughout all India, people have even been making pilgrimages to it, for crying out loud it is known as the heart of India.'

The man sat there looking bewildered.

'I knew nothing of it, we were greeted at the port, ushered straight into a hotel and instructed not to leave. The whole establishment had been hired out just for us but we were not allowed to go out, I did think it was a bit weird.'

'What was a bit weird?' asked Valla just beating George to the question.

'Well ... weird that it was financed privately. We was told a private individual was financing the whole operation himself, something about it he felt it was his duty. You must understand that we have been offered vast sums, with bonuses and even if we die it is guaranteed our families will still get the money. I am talking enough to be able to afford to not work again, if you were careful with it.'

'Confound him, whoever he is.' said George. 'What is his name?'

'We don't know.' The man responded.

'What did he look like?' asked Jayadev.

'I don't know, we do not know anything about him and fancy that was rather the point. We were given no freedom at all, we had everything we wanted, food, drink, entertainment, first class transport yet we did not converse with anyone outside our circle, as I said he even hired out the whole hotel.'

George and Valla looked at each other.

'Why would a man go to such lengths Vallabhendra?'

'That is what I cannot fathom George. I have been thinking about what you said earlier about it being perfectly timed. Did you know that the army is out on training manoeuvres this week? Nearly the entire unit, there is barely a scattering of personnel in the base at the moment.'

'This man whoever he is has done his homework meticulously, what do you think we should do Vallabhendra?'

'There is something else you should know.' The bleeding man interrupted.

'Oh what is that?' said Vallabhendra annoyed at being interrupted.

'We were given instructions not to kill you, everyone else was dispensable to be eliminated to ensure your capture or surrender.'

'What both of us?' asked Vallabhendra.

The man nodded.

Vallabhendra and George again looked at each other. The men who were gathered round watching including Jayadev tutted their disgust at what they had heard.

Without warning Vallabhendra pulled out his revolver and pressed it hard against the man's head. 'What's the plan?'

'*I will tell you all I know, I heard you talking just before I was attacked.* You are right we are coming through the dense jungle, a skirmish force was sent ahead to confuse and disorientate you. While you were distracted we silently took the hotel and rigged it with explosives, no easy feat, luckily the tigers in there were all old or ill ...'

Vallabhendra pulled back the hammer on his gun. George quickly smacked his arm out of the way as he knew Vallabhendra was about to pull the trigger. Vallabhendra stared at him but George just shook his head solemnly.

'What can I say Gentlemen *you wanted the truth.*'

'I suggest you omit any tiger killing out of the story unless it is key to our defence.' said Vallabhendra.

'I have to say Vallabhendra is right. I promise you if anyone manages to slay our great cat everyone will die today including you.' George said with the look of a million wars in his eyes.

The man gulped, the hitherto building confidence dropped back out of him. His blood drenched torn clothes were now starting to dry and began sticking to his skin like pieces of papier-mâché.

'We have not got him yet, what else can I say.'

'Oh we know that, now continue.' said George 'we haven't got all day.'

The man pulled a brief incredulous expression but wisely suppressed any comment about the fact that they had interrupted *him*.

'They are coming through the dense Jungle with elephants. They hope to shoot the tigers as they come, you won't have much longer.'

'How many?' asked Jayadev.

'About a hundred.' The man responded.

'*A hundred.*' responded Jayadev in a startled voice.

'Yes, thereabouts but we have lost about twenty men to tigers already.'

A brief smile crossed everyone's face.

'Why would they leave the road open, we can simply just walk off down it and escape.' asked Vallabhendra.

'Yes you could, I promise you it will work, someone actually pointed that out during the debrief, we were assured you would not run.'

Vallabhendra and George again exchanged puzzled looks. George scratched his head.

'I was trying to spy, my intention was to turn back any minute, I lost my colleague about ten minutes before I met you.'

The sound of a distant elephant was carried on a light breeze. It came from the direction of the dense jungle on the other side of the oval.

George stood up and searched the prisoner again, he found a hidden knife and threw it into the jungle.

'If you have been candid a fair trial awaits you, I will see to it. Your co-operation will be noted. Whether you hang or not is not for me to decide but I promise you that much. Jayadev come here please.'

Jayadev walked over.

'Yes George what would you like me to do.'

'I want you to escort this man at gunpoint down the road to the nearest village.'

Jayadev stood there, his face dropped.

'Don't look so crestfallen man, I know you want to help. We need this man alive he may still be of vital use. Besides, no man has any business killing an unarmed prisoner. I will also confess you have been weighing on my conscience ever since this whole saga began, it will not do to see you killed.' said George putting his hands on Jayadev's shoulder in a pleading manner.

'Jayadev, your father died with honour yes, but we will see that you *live* with honour, that is more respectful to his memory than anything.' said Vallabhendra.

'Your words are too kind.' Jayadev replied.

'So you will do me this favour?'

'For us.' said Vallabhendra.

'I will do as you ask, since it means so much to you.'

'If he tries any funny business whatsoever shoot him. Make sure you walk at least ten paces behind.'

'No need for that George.' said Vallabhendra signalling for the tiger to come over to him.

The tiger that had attacked the prisoner walked over and nuzzled Vallabhendra. Vallabhendra ruffled his fur and kissed his head.

'Jayadev come over here and greet this tiger.' said Vallabhendra.

Jayadev approached, the tiger was still nuzzling. Vallabhendra lifted the tigers head with both of his hands and looked it in the eye, he turned the tigers head toward Jayadev and motioned toward him.

The tiger looked up. Jayadev leant in to greet the tiger. Blood sprayed, Jayadev's head fell back just hanging on the spinal cord with a little flesh. The tiger had nearly the whole of his neck in its mouth. The tiger spat out Jayadev's neck.

'*How? How did you know? We gave you no clues, I barely even looked at him.*' squealed the prisoner.

'You have underestimated your quarry I'm afraid.' said George calmly. 'The only question we want to know is *why?*'

'Was he to assassinate us when we dropped our guard?' asked Vallabhendra kicking the man's leg to prompt him.

'*No*, everything is as I said. It still is. Jayadev was an insurance policy should you decide to flee, he was simply to stick with you and report where you were. You would have then been finished off. It didn't matter, in the long run you would have still lost everything.'

'We told you it was a lie about the army, so why didn't you come clean?' snapped George.

'When I realised he wasn't going to break character I saw there was a chance we might still get paid. He would certainly arrange for my escape or my employer would have bribed me out of trouble. Do you mind if I smoke?'

'Not at all.' said Vallabhendra gesturing with his hand.

The man pulled out a pack of cigarettes, wincing in pain as he did. Vallabhendra lent down and pulling out some tinder lit his cigarette for him. The prisoner inhaled deeply and blew out a thick cloud of smoke that hung around like jungle mist first thing in the morning.

'We did believe the story about the British Army, it seemed plausible at the time. We were also aware there was something else behind it, I mean, an individual spending such a vast, vast fortune. You don't need to be *Sherlock Holmes* to work out that there was more to it, but we did not know what that was.'

'Neither do *we*.' said Vallabhendra his cheeks flushing red.

'How did you know about Jayadev?'

George looked at Vallabhendra who motioned his hand back toward him.

'Why the Great Tiger King himself of course. When he first met Jayadev he sniffed him over and then lay down in front of him. I told Jayadev that when he doesn't like someone he growls and roars and I have to send the tiger away. What he did not know was that I was lying. He was in front of Jayadev to protect us *from him*.

Something else I withheld is that Palak knew someone who knew Arshad's son, he happened to mention that he was a woodsman. Myself and Vallabhendra live akin to woodsmen, as you see our hands are significantly calloused, yet when I shook his hand it was smooth, unblemished, even soft.

Further to that, upon seeing he was wearing a Jade pendant, I informed him that his father carried a Jade religious trinket and purposely added the word *always*. I wasn't sure whether he would fall for the ruse. I think he must have thought it was a stroke of fortune as he was wearing a piece of jade around his neck but again it was my own skullduggery.

His Father did indeed sacrifice himself to whatever Spirit or God he believed it was, but we only know that as he proudly wrote a message in the sandy dirt albeit his guns had also been purposely tossed aside.

I trusted my tiger's instinct and it now seemed to be paying off as it always did. I was curious to see what it was that he sensed. Immediately I envisaged he was trying to get close to me and propose a lucrative business plan or some other nefarious deed that would net him profit and lose me a fortune.

He also informed us that he came straight from the train, but he told Palak that he popped by to inspect the army base – they are in opposite directions. As soon as the mayhem started I knew he was involved somehow so I applied the old adage of keeping your enemies closer. I suspect that when he inspected the army base was the one time he actually told the truth, he did precisely that - he went to inspect the army base to ensure they had all left for the training exercise.

There was also the reaction to his father's death, he had no feeling toward me whatsoever. Even the most rational man would consider me responsible to some degree yet he held no animosity toward me whatsoever, he didn't even struggle to convey his supposed true feelings to me. The real man hates my guts by the way and has made it clear he never wants to see my face. I respect that so have not sought him out to make reparations although not all his good fortune in recent years is luck, as he supposes it to be.

There was one thing above all this that overshadowed your whole ruse from the start.'

'Oh what was that?' said their captive looking startled that there was yet more revelation to come.

George looked at the bleeding man with a curious look. 'The real son of Arshad does not speak any English at all!'

The prisoner looked bewildered and for a second even bemused then he dropped his head and nodded it in a defeatist manner.

'So Mr Stagsden.' said George opening the billfold he had taken out of the man's pockets earlier.

'You're so cleverly placed spy was in fact one of the worst spies known to history; we had him clocked within an hour.'

'So what now?' said Mr Stagsden looking up at George and Valla.

'I have been truthful, ok - I did not admit the truth about Jayadev but who would, if he was Vallabhendra would you give him up George, or visa-versa Vallabhendra?'

The prisoner looked at them both.

'Familiarity won't save you.' replied Vallabhendra.

George looked out onto the road and saw one of the tigers laying dead in a pool of blood that had poured from its chest.

George leant down to Jayadev's body and took the gun out of the dead man's belt, he opened it, checked it was loaded then snapped it shut again.

'Here,' said George throwing it in to the lap of the bleeding Mr Stagsden.

'What are you doing ... *no ... no ... wait please.*' Stagsden pleaded, his eyes open wide with terror.

'*Now you're armed.*' said George walking off.

The words were barely finished when George heard a horrendous slushy crunch as the tiger finished Mr Stagsden off.

The remaining party of men walked out onto the road, they heard the elephant again, it sounded closer than before.

'We need to act. Before we do gentleman I suggest we say a prayer. These people have nothing but murder planned that much is evident. The way out is down that road if you want to take it, he was telling the truth about *that*, that much I am sure of.' They gathered in a circle. 'I am a Christian, I know I do not appear to be spiritual but do not doubt my faith, I say this because I will pray for you as well.'

'And we will pray for you George.' said a slightly rotund man with parted hair.

After the men had finished praying in their various faiths Vallabhendra was the first person to break the silence.

'We will fight them in the jungle it will give us an advantage against those on elephants.'

George swung the bag off his shoulder and started handing out grenades.

'Use them sparingly. If you can, use them to scare the elephants, if we time it right they may even trample a few of their own men. Whatever you do, mind the tigers, they could be around.

I have the outline of a plan but with what we are facing and the amount of men we have it is not much. If anyone wants to say anything speak, I mean it, if you have a better plan or do not think something will work please tell us.'

'Tell us your plan.' said Valla putting his hand on his friend's shoulder.

'I am thinking, depending on how much time we have, that we will spread out and walk into the jungle to try to find somewhere with a good view ahead so we can have some long shots. If we can set up, have our rifles ready with a steady shot from a good vantage point and if every man makes his shot count straight, we should be able to take down a fair few. We have the element of surprise, I am hoping that they will be overconfident in their success. As all this is occurring I will get the Tigers to come in from the sides.'

'It's an ambush.' said one of the men.

'Precisely. Do not get too excited they could come from any direction. I think it will happen as we have been informed yet you must be prepared for the unexpected. Be confident in your shots but not in the outcome, remember we will be heavily outnumbered and outgunned. I promise you one thing Gentlemen it will be smart thinking that saves lives and wins the day, nothing else.'

'Sounds like a good plan to me George, remember the tigers are our friends, our family, one of us. If you see one in danger protect it like you would each other.' said Vallabhendra.

'Yes and don't forget they have been protecting you all day.' added George.

'They are our kin, we are the Tiger People.' said one of the men.

'If I had some whisky I would drink to that.' replied George.

'So would I' said Vallabhendra holding up an imaginary drink.

'We shall all drink well tonight, but I need you to be silent for a minute.'

All the men fell silent. George cupped his hands around his mouth and let out the strangest sound, it sounded just like a tigers call. The men looked startled. Vallabhendra smiled knowingly.

The tigers that were hiding in the trees leapt out of the canopy, other tigers that were either in hiding or waiting came running from every direction pouring out of the jungle and on to the road like an exodus of rats.

George stood there waiting patiently like a father after calling his children home from play. They stood in front of him and roared, the jungle screamed once again with the sound of fleeing birds and squealing primates.

The roars died, the tigers sat upright like pupils in a classroom. George motioned through the compound to the jungle on the other side. He pointed to the cats and putting his hands together motioned for them to go either way so they would approach from the side into the jungle opposite. Without command the tiger's all stood. George roared a tigers roar as loud as he could and waved the Tigers away in opposite directions with one strong swipe of his two hands.

George picked up his rifle and held it high in the air, *'For the land of tooth and claw – long live the tiger, long live India, long reign the Great Tiger King!'*

'For the land of tooth and claw' the men chanted.

George still holding his rifle jogged into the compound and through to the other side. Vallabhendra ran beside him, all of the other men fanned out so they were running across the great courtyard in a straight line.

'Stop here.' said George now in full military command.

'What was your rank?' asked one of the men.

'Rank is not important I lead out of experience nothing else, remember what I said fan out but keep within hand signalling distance on either side of me or Vallabhendra. Use your ammo sparingly. You should need rifles only at first, get as many long shots as you can and remember do not panic. Make every shot count. If we ensure that every bullet we fire hits someone we definitely have a chance. I am pretty certain they have underestimated the amount of tigers that are with us.

Should any of you fall I will ensure that your families are looked after and that you are buried or cremated with honour. Of course we shall all live. Let's go to war men.'

They fanned out as they walked heading for different entrances into the jungle. They had gone about twenty paces when without warning a huge trumpeting Elephant with three armed men atop burst out of the jungle.

Out of the corner of their eye the men saw a gigantic orange blur come bolting out of its hiding place, the Great Tiger King in all his majesty ran full pelt covering the earth with giant strides, the muscles bulging like giant pistons powering the true king of beasts, claws out ploughing the earth, baring it's teeth, the giant swords of death, within seconds it was airborne, the king of all cats, the largest tiger ever known to man was flying through the air.

George snapped up his rifle and in a split second sent the first man a bullet through the forehead. The tiger took all three of men down to the ground and before they could even contemplate the great cat tore them all asunder. The men moved aside and let the lightly scratched Elephant through.

'*Do not deviate men, forward and quicker than ever.*' shouted George

The men continued veering off toward the jungle, along with the great tiger king and George and Valla. The long row of men all glanced at each other as they entered at different intervals.

The jungle was silent, still. There was not a sound, the men looked round at each other, George signalled to advance forward. They crept forward still not a sound.

'It's weird Vallabhendra, after that elephant I was expecting to encounter them immediately.'

'Are you thinking *we are the ones* who are walking into an ambush?'

'I am not sure.'

'Well let us keep on walking.' said Vallabhendra moving forward with his rifle poised.

Twenty paces later George, raised his hand and the party stopped. He listened carefully.

'Do you hear that Valla?'

'What George, I can't hear anything.'

'Listen carefully.'

The men stood there for a few seconds and listened, on the faint breeze a noise travelled their way, it was distant and sounded like something large moving through the jungle. You could faintly hear branches, trees and plants breaking.

'*It's them.*' said Valla.

'I know.' George replied, 'Come on.' He said waving the party forward. 'Look ahead Vallabhendra, there is a small clearing with some fallen logs that should give us some cover.'

'Perfect.' replied Valla.

As they approached George stopped the party and indicated to the men that this was where they were going to make their stand. He instructed them to find cover, a place where they could set up a steady aim. On his first shot they were to fire, carefully picking off the men on elephant back first. When they got close they were to use grenades but with caution. He conveyed all this with military sign language, which for the most part the men seemed to grasp.

He also indicated to the men that they should use large leaves and small branches to disguise their outline. The men signalled their acknowledgment and feverishly set about their business. Some were lucky to have an almost hide like set naturally created for them by the jungle, others like George and Valla had an excellent firing position but risked being spotted. The log they were about to use was large and the clearing beyond it enabled them to see far ahead. The location was so good that George contemplated bringing all the men behind that one log but that would not do, expect the unexpected.

Vallabhendra pulled out a large machete and upon finding some smaller branches hacked them off at the trunk so he had a mini tree in his hand. He cut down four and asked George to get in position then he laid the branches with its leaves and smaller branches over him, to give George full cover. Vallabhendra then got down next to George and pulled the other two branches over himself.

George looked down the line of men and saw them mimicking Vallabhendra's actions. George then looked ahead and in the far distance he saw the tree's starting to shimmer.

'They're coming Vallabhendra get ready.' George said as he turned and signalled the men lined up on his side. Vallabhendra did likewise to the men lined away from him.

'*Where's the bloody cat gone George?*' They both turned their heads and looked behind them but the great tiger king was nowhere to be seen.

'He picks his moments doesn't he George?'

'That he does Vallabhendra, I'm glad *he* doesn't need moral support.' cackled George.

The men sniggered.

An elephant trumpeted, the trees continued to shimmer in the distance, an Elephant suddenly appeared out of the dense jungle waving its trunk, then another and another. They were fanned out in a line and walking straight toward them. Men walked between the elephants with more and more pouring from the thick jungle.

Vallabhendra had his sights lined up.

'I have the one at the front steering the Elephant.' said George.

'I have the elephant to the left.' replied Vallabhendra.

The elephants noisily continued stomping through the undergrowth clearing a path through the jungle as they went. When they reached the opposite end of the clearing a man put up his hand and the party stopped.

'Vallabhendra cover us well I think he has a spyglass.'

Vallabhendra and George pulled the branches tight over themselves. They could just make out the man lifting something to his eye and looking around.

'I reckon he is suspicious George, he senses a trap.'

'He can suspect all he likes Vallabhendra he doesn't actually know, and as long as that is the case we should retain the element of surprise. It does tell us something though.'

'What is that then?'

'That he knows the jungle well, there are many clearings, yet to stop so cautiously he must know he is approaching the compound.'

'Good point, our enemy is both smarter and more cunning than either of us has given them credit for.'

'You might be right there, still we need them to get closer if we are going to make every shot count.'

The man up ahead took the spyglass down from his eye and stood there eyeing the way ahead with great suspicion.

For a minute George and Vallabhendra thought they had been spotted but after a tense thirty seconds or so the man lifted his hand and raised it forward.

The party marched forth. As they started getting closer George and Vallabhendra saw the man gesture with his hands, the men raised their guns to an attack position upon seeing this gesture.

George was examining the party leader studiously, taking in everything, what he looked like, what weapons he was carrying, his current position, what his exact role might be. A flash of orange moving slowly through the undergrowth caught George's attention out of the corner of his eye.

'Vallabhendra get ready, the tigers are moving in just as I had hoped.'

'Why can't people just let them be?'

'Well we will make them regret messing with these tigers that I promise you.'

'Yes, yes we will George. So you're taking the leader?'

'Vallabhendra, the honour is yours if you want it.'

'Why thank you George, don't mind if I do. Who are you going for?'

'The man steering the lead elephant, we need to cover the tigers as much as we can.'

They came closer, George watched as one of the tigers ran out of nowhere and leapt through the air at the men on the lead elephant. George let out his shot, the driver fell, the tiger had already brought down the other men. There was another shot as Vallabhendra silenced the man yelling commands. He fell straight to the jungle floor.

The jungle came alive with gunshots as everyone opened fire. Tigers leapt out from the cover of the jungle, pulling the attacking men from the backs of their elephants. Any men on the ground who were not dropping from gunfire were getting savaged by the cats. But the tigers started falling as well, they watched in horror as one leapt at a man and received a mighty gunshot straight into its head, several of the men on elephants also found their mark.

'Bringing the elephants was a good idea, I'll give them that.' said George.

'But not good enough.' replied Vallabhendra as his rifle spoke, bringing down one of the men who was aiming at a tiger.

There was a mighty explosion, George and Vallabhendra saw two tigers hurled helplessly against the trees, torn to shreds by shrapnel.

'They have grenades.' said Vallabhendra as another explosion rang out.

The gunshots continued, more men were brought down. The element of surprise had been lost. The enemy was starting to take cover, tigers dispersed as more grenades were thrown. The battle was still too far out of range to use their own grenades but for now they had a stead fast position. As George and Vallabhendra fired several more shots they received precisely aimed return fire. The tree trunk they were hiding behind took a volley of shots, forcing George and Vallabhendra to duck behind it.

'They've clocked our location, we need to be vigilant.' said Vallabhendra.

'It took them a while they must not have known what hit them.' said George leaning up and taking a couple of shots.

The jungle fell eerily quiet, there was no sound, both parties had stopped exchanging fire.

George and Valla laid there behind the log for a second, both in their own thoughts reloading, double checking their ammo and that their back up weapons were still in place. They heard a man's scream.

George and Vallabhendra looked up over the log and saw one of the tigers leap through the air onto a mercenary, but as it savaged him another soldier came and shot the tiger multiple times, as he did George and Vallabhendra dropped him with a volley of shots.

All hell broke loose again, gunfire rattled from both sides and for the first time grenades were thrown towards them but fell short. Dust, debris, smoke and wood bark flew through the air, creating a miasmic collage.

Valla looked to the side, as he did he saw one of their men take a shot straight in the chest. It punched him so hard that he flew off his feet with blood spurting in an arc as his body flipped vertical, he landed with a heavy thud on his back.

'We have our first man down George, at least their wasting grenades.' said Vallabhendra firing another shot.

'Vallabhendra you're a genius, they are not wasting the grenades they are using the smoke to advance,' George said turning and signalling to the other men that they were being advanced upon, bullets were still dancing all around him.

The smoke cleared and they saw that some men had indeed advanced. There was a mighty trumpet from a huge bull elephant as it came charging through the jungle screaming in terror, it was heading straight for Vallabhendra and George.

'Uh, Vallabhendra.'

'I see it George, what shall we do?'

'Too late, *evacuate*.'

They both got up as the thunderous creature came stomping through, as they stood they immediately took a multitude of shots from every direction, they dived on the floor for cover.

'Damn it.' said George rolling over.

'*George you've been hit.*' cried Vallabhendra.

'I know.' He said going into his webbing and pulling out a homemade medical kit.

'Here, my friend let me have a look.' said Vallabhendra. 'It's ok it is a flesh wound, the bullet has passed through the outside of your arm.'

Vallabhendra took the bandage and started dressing his arm.

'Be quick man we haven't got time.' said George.

'Stay still you bugger.' said Vallabhendra as he quickly wrapped the bandage around George's arm. Vallabhendra was fastening the bandage with a pin when a man came over the log, before Vallabhendra knew what had happened George pulled the revolver out of his holster and shot the would be assailant in the head. There was a loud noise, they heard men scrambling to action, a huge orange flash shot out of the tree right above them and the men were no more.

'*Crafty bugger*, he was up the tree looking over us the whole time.' said George.

'Sneaky sod.' replied Vallabhendra laughing. The two men suddenly locked eyes and leapt to their feet.

The great tiger king was charging straight for a man.

'*Get back here you bloody stupid cat.*' yelled George at the top of his lungs.

'George, *they're going to get him.*'

George and Vallabhendra lifted up their guns and fired at the man the great tiger king was pursuing. There was a mighty explosion as several well placed grenades exploded, the great tiger king was thrown through the air, slammed against a tree and fell lifeless into some long grass.

'*They've killed our cat.*' screamed Vallabhendra pulling out his revolver and firing it with rage, bullets were already flying at them though and George pulled him back down behind cover, a bullet just missing his head as he did so.

'They have killed him.'

'I know Vallabhendra, *I know.*' said George. The two men looked at each with moist bloodshot eyes.

The firing continued, it seemed more purposeful, lone singular shots rang out.

'Something is not right why aren't they firing at us George, the bullets are not even close.'

They looked up and saw a tiger fall, then another.

'*Good God*, look Vallabhendra snipers have climbed the trees they are killing our tigers.'

'I fear we may up against worthy opponents after all.'

'Vallabhendra we have to save the tigers.'

George stood up whistled in either direction. He could see their men waving, one had been shot in the arm. George pointed out the snipers in the trees and informed them they were to go in to close quarters combat and as soon as they had a clear shot to use grenades.

Just as he was about to give the order the man nearest George and Vallabhendra was shot in the head by a single sniper shot.

George lifted his rifle and dashed through the open to a tree. Vallabhendra did the same but ran across the clearing, the other men all charged forward.

George leaned around the trunk and fired at a sniper in the tree, he missed, but as the man fired back Vallabhendra took him out. The man fell clumsily down the tree, cart wheeling through the branches.

George gave Vallabhendra a thumbs up, Vallabhendra responded by pointing out another sniper, Vallabhendra immediately fired a quick rushed shot that inevitably missed. The sniper lined Vallabhendra up in his sights and was immediately taken out by George's bullet.

George looked around, he could see dead tigers laying everywhere from both grenades and snipers. Tears filled his eyes and for a brief second he had to fight to bring himself from breaking down. He looked across and saw that Vallabhendra was having a similar experience.

A bullet ricocheted off the trunk just missing George's head, he turned with eyes full of hatred and lifted his rifle to an immediate clean shot. As he was about to pull the trigger, he lowered the barrel and shot just below, hitting the trunk and completely missing the sniper. George quickly hid back behind the tree, he looked across to Vallabhendra and indicated for Vallabhendra not kill him. Then George motioned to Vallabhendra to look around the other side of his trunk toward the tree, Vallabhendra did so and saw a huge tiger stalking their would be target.

Vallabhendra took a shot, missing the sniper completely, the bullet landing about two feet above the man's head in a thick branch. George waited about ten seconds and took another awfully aimed shot. The sniper not sure who to go for, raised his gun at George, George stepped about from behind the tree and held his rifle in the air. As the sniper was about to pull the trigger the tiger leapt and the man was no more.

There was an explosion to their left, all the men had advanced some on both sides without Vallabhendra and George. After checking for more snipers George and Vallabhendra ran forward, they came across dead bodies of the enemy who had been clawed and eaten by tigers or cut down by bullets. The gunfire ceased for a second, George was uneasy, like it was *them* who were now walking into a trap.

He saw the body of the leader laying on the ground, he went over and inspected the body, he was clean shaven with surprisingly long blonde hair, George looked at the man closely but did not recognise him. He searched and found a map of the compound and a rough sketch of their attack plan which hitherto had been foiled, he was Scandinavian but there was nothing that would explain a connection to himself. George quickly guessed that this was not the man behind it all.

More elephants came charging through from the deep jungle and all hell was let loose once again, the trap had been sprung. Mercenaries appeared from everywhere, violent gunfire was quickly exchanged. George ran forward and threw a grenade as hard he could, it worked perfectly, the grenade exploded by a tree adjacent to one of the elephants.

The elephant reared up squealing, as it did it charged forward and George heard a scream as it ran right through a couple of mercenaries crushing them to death instantly. It reminded George of the sound one gets when you step on a snail, for a moment he felt ill.

George was forced to dive to the ground, but he kept on crawling forward. He got up on one knee took someone out with a shot and ducked again, as he did a grenade landed right next to him. Immediately he picked it up and threw back, it exploded, a man screamed.

Grenades were now been heavily exchanged, he turned and saw Vallabhendra in a heavy fire fight, then he saw a wave of tigers coming in *'Push forward.'* George yelled running forward and taking three men out with his revolver. He threw three well placed grenades. George turned to see another of their men take a fatal bullet. George ran to help Vallabhendra but was held back, he saw some of their men coming to assist.

Tigers leapt through the air and smoke, men screamed, tigers growled, soldiers and cats fell. Smoke began to fill the jungle, a bullet hit one of the elephants and it charged forward.

'Watch out.' screamed George to the man on his left. It was too late, a giant elephant appeared out of the grey smoke and trampled the man to death.

'Confound it.' snapped George.

George was now crouching, the battle zone was too close for his rifle, he had out his revolver. Smoke was whirling everywhere trapped between the trees. George saw someone up ahead, he fired a shot the man fired back but missed.

George repeated but the man was as quick in response forcing them both to take cover. George leant against a tree and reloaded even though he had only spent a couple of rounds. The men both looked round at the same time and George got a good look at his opponent.

The man with short black hair and five o clock shadow stared at George with a ferocious grimace, it did not phase

George he knew that they key to surviving war was to remain calm, panic got you killed. His opponent was hunched behind a rock, George attempted a steady shot at some shoulder that was sticking out from behind the rock, he missed. His opponent replied with a volley of shots, it was then George realised that his assailant had two hand guns.

As he once again took refuge behind the large trunk George's senses heightened. He snapped his gun around to find an Indian man with a tuft of hair on his chin looking at him, it was one of the men from his team, Depali.

The man looked at George and snuck up behind a neighbouring tree, he motioned to George that he would use a grenade. George had two left himself. He communicated back that they would both hold and throw their grenades on his count.

George pulled the pin but did not throw it, the man look concerned, they waited about ten seconds, then George threw his on one side of the rock and Depali threw his on the other. The plan was executed perfectly because they had held the grenades before throwing them, they exploded before landing obliterating their enemy hidden behind the rock. They waited a second in case.

'He is dead you can be rest assured of that Depali.' said George coming out from the cover of the tree. 'Glad you stopped by.'

Depali laughed. 'I thought you might be.'

Depali stepped out from behind the tree and joined George. George checked his arm the bleeding had stopped, he put his rifle down by the tree and snapped open his revolver.

'Did you just hear something Depali?' George said.

'No, what did you hear?'

'I am not sure ... a weird noise, never mind.'

'How many do you think are left out there George?'

'I am not sure, I think that there might be some stragglers.'

'We have lost a lot of tigers.'

'I know, I can't stand it, I ...' as George was loading the bullets in his gun, a weird shaped stone by the side of Depali's leg caught his attention. He looked at it again it was more like a small black rock, the shape was peculiar it was oval.

'*Dep ...*' George screamed, he did not get chance to finish his sentence. The grenade exploded. George was sent flying violently through the air slamming his back against the tree that he had just been hiding behind. His gun flew out of his hand, he fell to the floor the wind knocked out him.

George, quickly tried to clear his eyes, looking across he saw that the grenade had literally blown Depali to pieces. Blood and bits of his body were plastered across the other tree. George heard the click of a hammer being pulled back. He looked up and saw a white man, with bright blue eyes and long blonde hair. He had two plats of hair coming from the back, drooping over his shoulders and down his chest over his black shirt. George was tempted to laugh, but this man wore the face of a remorseless killer, an expression that George had seen many times before.

'You have killed many of my friends.' The man said lifting the barrel.

George with typical stoicism smiled at his aggressor. 'Well, why don't you meet one of mine.'

The shiny gold blade of the ceremonial dagger went straight through the man's throat with ease. He dropped the gun and went to put his hand around his throat, as he did the blade was pulled out, blood spurted everywhere, the man fell clutching his throat desperately trying stop the blood but it was no use, the man fell silent to the ground.

'Well that was good timing Vallabhendra, I must say.'

'Sorry I could not get here earlier my friend I had my own preoccupations as you can imagine, *George your leg.*'

George looked down and saw a large piece of shrapnel in his leg he pulled it out, blood oozed forth, George winced.

'Confound that bloody grenade, they killed Depali.'

'I see that my friend, we can grieve for the fallen later, how deep is your wound?'

'I will be fine it is just muscle.' said George getting up.

Vallabhendra helped him up. 'I am alright Vallabhendra don't fuss. George ripped some cloth from his shirt and tied it around his leg. He lifted his leg a couple of times.

'It will be fine until I get back, a little sore but I can move around still. You could pass my gun though the blast threw it from my hand, it's down there.'

Vallabhendra leant over, picked up the gun and passed it to George.

George again snapped the barrel open and continued reloading his revolver.

'We have all fought valiantly here today George a battle to go down in history I reckon.'

A loud bang filled the air and a bullet punched Vallabhendra's shoulder, then another one hit his leg, finally one punched him straight in the gut. The great man fell back, George snapped his gun shut as the assailant was bringing the gun around to him. George confidently walked forward, his gun speaking with every step, the bullets thudded into the man's chest, violently jolting him backwards with every shot. The bullets ran out but such was his rage that he kept on firing, repeatedly clicking empty.

He stopped for a second looking at the man laying dead on the jungle floor, for a minute he wished he could come back to life so he could shoot him again. George turned around to tend to Vallabhendra but a large man with a handlebar moustache stepped out of the bushes. The gun in the assailants hand was not even raised when a tiger sprang from nowhere and tore him asunder.

George finally rushed over to Vallabhendra's side.

'Let me have a look.' said George lifting up Vallabhendra's shirt, the wound was bleeding heavily, George pulled out a clean pad from his first aid kit.

'You're going to be alright old boy, hold this pad tight, it is bleeding but the blood is not dark, that is a good sign. How are you feeling?'

'Like I have been shot three times.' said Vallabhendra managing a small smile.

'Glad to see your humour is not lost. Now listen, we need to get you urgent medical attention, the battle is over for you my friend, I will catch you up. You will live my friend you have to.' said George his eye's moistening up as he did so.

The tiger came over and started nuzzling Vallabhendra, it looked concerned. George stood up and whistled loudly, several tigers appeared he listened and after a commotion in the bushes and few more presented themselves.

Upon seeing Vallabhendra they all lined up and lay down in front of him.

George pointed to Vallabhendra and the direction of the nearest village. As if they were all conversing in some fluent human cat language, the tigers ran forward and by grabbing swathes of clothing in their mouths, picked up Vallabhendra and ran off with him at full speed.

George watched as Vallabhendra rapidly disappeared from view as they ran across the clearing. All George could see was Vallabhendra's face poking out the end of a line of tigers. George waved solemnly *'Good luck old man.'* he heard Vallabhendra shout.

'Keep pressure on it.' was George's response.

George stood there examining his own wounds, his clothes now just a torn collage of dirt and blood yet he was strong and in good shape, yes he would finish the job.

He looked at the tigers. 'Shall we finish this my friends?' he said to them.

There was the sound of a twig snapping, the cats spun their heads, George aimed his *Webley.* A familiar figure came walking through.

'I tell you one thing Zubhasamanvit you might not be able light a fire but you can sure fight a war.'

'I heard your whistle George.'

'Where is everyone else?'

'I think they're all dead, I can't believe we're still standing, we have come so far.'

'I fear they have won my friend whatever the outcome.'

'Why do you say that?'

'Because after this the great tiger kingdom will be no more, so in one sense they have achieved their goal.'

'But *they* won't be around to enjoy it.'

'Exactly.' replied George.

Out of nowhere Palak suddenly appeared.

'By Jove, Palak you came strolling through like you're on a Sunday afternoon stroll.'

'Hello George, you whistling at the top of your voice doesn't exactly invite caution, you look like you have seen some action.'

'Just taken a couple of knocks is all.'

'I think we got nearly all of them, from what I can see.' said Zubhasamanvit.

'Good then I want you both to go home.'

Palak who did not have a scratch on him, flicked his braided ponytail angrily over his shoulder. 'Why? It is not finished George, look at you, you are covered in blood and I am in tip top condition.'

'Look enough people have died already whoever this maniac is, I am sure he is still alive. I can feel it in my gut, I still have tigers, but this man I will face alone, I am a man honour, a man of the gentry and if it is a duel that this man wants then that is what he will have.

Too many people have died today for two of you to live is more than I realistically could have hoped for considering the numbers that we were facing.

Vallabhendra has been shot three times including once in the gut, get to his side that is the only thing I will ask of you. Take two tigers with you just in case, you will be handsomely rewarded whatever happens.' George said rechecking his weapons including the knife on his hip.

'We fight by you because you are our friend George, damn you, you're not the only one who loves these tigers and cares about them.' shouted Palak hotly, Zubhasamanvit was nodding in agreement.

'That was not what I meant I am asking you a favour as a friend but I am your employer and that is why you will be rewarded. Even if I was not your employer you would still be rewarded as our tiger has serendipitously been very profitable so we will all take a share. Of course most will go to the cats in any way I can get it to them.

Listen my friends, this is something I need to do alone. If I die, knowing that you two and Vallabhendra survived will make me a lot happier. Besides that Vallabhendra may still need you.'

'I don't like it George, we are not certain how many are left there may be a load more adversaries out there if all we know.' said Palak.

George just stood there with an impertinent look on his face.

'We can see you are not going to back down. Where is Vallabhendra?' asked Zubhasamanvit.

'The tigers have taken him to the village.' replied George.

'Ok we will get there as soon as we can.' said Zubhasamanvit.

'Good luck George.' said Palak.

'Yes, good luck to the both of you.'

'I will be fine just get to that village and do not come back regardless of whether I return or not. Godspeed my friends.'

George clicked his fingers, two of the tigers immediately got up and started walking behind Palak and Zubhasamanvit.

After watching them disappear, George called out the tiger's roar, the jungle once again burst to life. Tigers appeared from everywhere. George was astounded how many tigers came out from hiding he had feared that they were all dead, if not certainly most of them. The tigers swarmed around him, he also knew whether there would be those that were out of earshot, it eased the pain.

As the tigers sat around him George smiled to himself, there were more tigers than enemy left by a long way that much he was sure of, he motioned for the tiger's to go out and hunt remaining soldiers out and then to return to him.

The tigers ran through the jungle at full speed. George stood there listening intently with his revolver at his side. He heard the first scream, then a gunshot, another man screamed, more gunshots, an explosion, yet more screaming.

Like when popcorn cooks and all the kernels have nearly popped so the sounds of death became intermittent, more drawn out until there was an eerie silence.

Tigers started reappearing out of the jungle and returning to George, many with blood on their mouths and claws. Finally George was sure that all that would return had done so.

George stood there looking at his beloved cats, tears filled his eyes. He held them back, he knew what he had to do. The result was now inevitable no government would allow this battle to go unnoticed, as insignificant as it was the fear of uprising would be too great. The only thing he could do was save the tigers, he knew no matter how much he talked and bartered in the end the simplest way would be for the army to cull them.

'*My cats ... my tigers ... my friends ... my children!* These are morose times for us all, no longer can we be together. They have destroyed us, they have murdered The Great Tiger King himself.' George choked back tears and took a deep breath. 'We have no choice I cannot stand to watch you perish, I would rather witness my own demise.

You are the true rulers of earth, judges of the forest, tamer of the wild, the true king of the jungle, now go, establish and rule your own kingdoms, each one of you.'

A solitary tear slid reluctantly down George's cheek. The tigers all swarmed around him nuzzling him.

'No. no, no, *no!*' shouted George flicking them away with his hand, *'Now Go,'* he screamed, lunging at them as if he was about to attack. The tigers all fled some stopped and looked back but again he waved them off.

He was now all alone in the jungle, his expression changed from one of sadness to one of rage and malice. He again checked all his guns and that his knife was easily accessible.

The grenades had set off fires, the jungle was a mix of smoke and haze, the eerie silence heightened his senses. George started to walk. He pushed aside giant leaves, stepped over fallen trunks, he started coming across the dead bodies of both men and feline. He was sure that his persecutor was still alive and waiting for him.

Like a moth drawn to a flame George knew he could not resist the temptation. The unspoken invite that would reveal the great mystery. George wanted his revenge that was for sure.

A faint sound carried in the smoke reached George's ears. It was a soft groan like that of someone writhing in pain. George stopped and listened, upon hearing the faint noise again he trod cautiously towards it. Several minutes later he came upon patch of grass with a litter dead bodies spread across it, one was moving.

George ran over, it was an enemy soldier that had been shredded by both grenade and tiger.

'You w ... won't win, kill me it will make no difference, he is waiting for you.'

'I am not going to kill you fiend you are unarmed and injured, just tell me who it is, who is behind all of this?'

The man coughed up a load of blood and spat it out on the ground, with a blood coated chin he said '*No one knows, he was one of us, the whole time he was one of us, hiding in with ...*' The man coughed up again '*with the soldiers. It was not personal for me ... it was just a job.*'

'I forgive you brother. I am a soldier also. Die in peace.'

'The man tried to grab Georges hand but didn't have the strength. '*His name is ... his nam ...*' The man's eyes opened wide and he breathed his last.

George got up and with his revolver facing everywhere he looked he checked the perimeter, there was no obvious signs as to where his elusive guest was hiding.

George moved on further into the battlefield, the pit of his stomach winding tighter and tighter at every dead tiger he came across. The silence had returned, not a monkey calling, a bird singing or a deer barking, even the insects were silent as if the whole Jungle was holding a silence to commemorate the fallen. George cautiously watched his step trying to be as silent as he could. The smoke wisped through the jungle like cobwebs. George could hear his own heart beating faster and faster.

He considered looking for the body of the Great Tiger King but decided against it. He must deal with this fiend and exact revenge then he could tend to the dead. George tried to think like his enemy, where would *he* hide? What was the guarantee that they would find each other, the jungle is dense and big. It crossed George's mind that perhaps his persecutor was waiting at the compound. The chances were high that there is where George would retreat to and therefore the perfect place for an ambush.

As he pondered this he stepped over a dead tiger and into a small clearing, the smoke had cleared some, he could see a body on the floor, it was one of his own soldiers. Misty smoke concealed the other end of the clearing like some mysterious entrance to a cave.

George rushed over and turned over the body. It was one of his men, George held his head down for a second, the man's eyes were still open, he closed them, as he did so he heard a voice.

'Hello George.'

George looked up to see a tall, lithe man step out of the mist, the face so familiar the gaunt sunken eyeballs, the stretched skin, the receding dark greyish hairline. It was Charles.

'Good God. Charles it cannot be, you are dead, confound you man you are dead.'

'Yes, Charles is dead.'

George stepped forward there was a different look in the man's eyes, yet his face and build were the same, it was Charles. George noticed the gun trained on him as he examined the man closer and began to see almost unnoticeable differences, a mole in the wrong place, something about his gait. At last George realised the truth.

'You know it is a strange thing but in all the years I knew Charles he never once mentioned that his brother Henry was a twin.'

'Very good George, he always said you were a quick study.'

'This is all about your brother?'

'Come, come George you killed him, he was my twin brother and you killed him of course I am going to avenge him and now at last I am going to kill you.' The man remained icily calm as he said it.

'I didn't bloody kill him you madman, he was killed by a tiger.'

'Do you know how long I have dreamed of this moment, the years I have spent laying awake at night carefully, methodically planning my revenge and now here we are. All your friends are dead, your compound and hotel destroyed, your tigers scattered to the wind plus the very fact that you know you are you about to die. Please try and savour it with me just for a second, the delicious taste of retribution.

You did kill him, you killed him when you abandoned him, when you chose a tiger *over him*, you were the only one with the power to stop it but you didn't.'

'*I did not know what was about to happen did I, I didn't know, he was my friend, I have grieved all these years over his loss, if only I could go back but I can't can I? No I was not following him do you know why, because he was obsessed, he became a blood thirsty lunatic that day, like you have become now look at yourself you bloody great fool, you think your brother would approve?*'

'It is amusing to hear you say that, do you know how I financed all this? My brother left me everything in his will. If I was not alive it was to go to you, I find it a delicious irony that you were second to inherit yet I spent it all on destroying you.'

'It is clear to me that albeit he was your twin you did not know him in the slightest. Yes Charles could be a mad obstinate fool but if it had not have cost him his life I assure you he would have seen sense. He would have even been contrite about it especially the needless deaths that had occurred by then.'

'Well it matters not as soon you'll be dead and I still have plenty of money left to ensure that neither you, your kingdom or your tigers are ever remembered.'

'So you are still a wealthy man eh? Good, then you can afford to pay for your funeral.' The second the word funeral left Georges mouth he brought up his wrist and fired.

Henry was taken by surprise, he immediately returned fire, the men stood blankly shooting at each other for a second then they both leapt to the trees for cover.

'*You'll never kill me George.*'

'*We'll see about that Henry.*' chuckled George, he knew arrogance was often someone's undoing. George spun around and took a shot he hit the tree right next to Henry's head.

'Good shot old man, but not good enough.' said Henry firing his gun and changing tree as he did.

The bullets missed but George was listening to the sounds in the background, Henry was moving from tree to tree trying to flank him. George cut across to try and out flank him and get on his six. Henry suddenly realising what was going on turned and fired several times, George just managed to get to cover, it was a narrow miss and they both knew it.'

'Getting closer George ha ... ha ... ha ...'

'You sir are nothing short of a mad dog and I will gladly put you down.'

'How when I am the terror of the trees.' came the reply as Henry's gun spoke yet again.

'More like pillock in the plants.' George mused to himself. He heard Henry make a run for it and stepped out firing every shot of his revolver at him as he ran, now it was Henry's turn for a near miss. George stayed still for a minute and closed his eyes thinking of a way to bring this to a quick conclusion they would be here all day the way they were circling each other through the trees.

George decided to move in closer so he ran to a tree nearer Henry, again they were both behind a tree about twenty feet apart. George stepped out at the same time as Henry and fired, the gun clicked empty. George looked at his revolver incredulous how had he forgotten to reload?

'I believe they call this check mate.' said Henry.

George wasted no time, he threw the revolver right at Henry's face. Henry lifted his hand to cover it but needing more time than that would give him George pulled out his last grenade and hurled it at Henry. The pin was still in but Henry did not have time to notice as soon as he had blocked the two objects thrown at him and started to bring down his arm to shoot, George was upon him.

George punched him straight in the face Henry flew to the ground dropping his gun, he got up and charged George. The men grappled. George was elbowed in the face, but got in a few punches, the men rolled away from each other and leapt to their feet.

'You will not win George.' Henry screamed.

'Your confidence does not scare me.' replied George.

The men charged at each other, they began boxing for a while almost as if it were a match, their faces becoming bloody and bruised. George feigned a slip and as he stumbled forward Henry threw a massive punch but that was George's intention, cleverly he dodged it and launched a powerful counterpunch. It caught Henry off guard and he went stumbling back.

George followed up with some really hard punches in quick succession then with all his might he leapt up and kicked Henry in the chest.'

Henry slammed into the trunk of a tree and slid down the bark bleeding and half conscious. George spotted Henry's gun on the ground, he quickly picked it up.

Henry started to come to, he saw George standing there with a gun trained on him and realised his predicament.

'Are you going to murder me like you did my brother?'

'I did not murder your brother and after this I shall grieve for him no more.'

'What are you waiting for George pull the trigger?'

George looked at the bloodied and bruised man laying on the floor in front of him, he saw the face of his deceased friend looking back at him, all the pain and trouble that had been caused. Even all the events of the great war had not prepared him for a situation such as this.

George could not help but beam a huge smile as he spotted something out of the corner of his eye.

'Kill me you bastard, like my brother when you murdered him.'

'I did not murder you brother,' George screamed. 'I am glad that you mention him though, I will not murder you on the contrary I will allow you to have your revenge.'

Henry looked up at George, his gaunt face riddled with curiosity. 'You will let me kill you?'

George mopped his brow with his blooded dirty handkerchief. 'No I will not, as I have already said I did not kill your brother.'

'Then what on earth do you mean?'

'You want to murder your brother's killer so badly that you have killed many innocent people, many innocent creatures and ruined thousands of people's lives.' Georges face grew redder and redder as his recently deceased friends flashed before him. *'You want revenge that badly, you really want to avenge your brother's death, well be my guest if you can, there is your brother's murderer, there you go*

MURDER HIM!' screamed George pointing at the jungle to their left.

There walking slowly towards them was the Great Tiger King himself as big as ever his paws treading down more foliage than George's size eleven boots, he was looking dirty and dishevelled but with the exception of a few scratches was otherwise fine. The faded scar on his leg still showing proud.

Henry gulped loudly.

'Your brother killed the tigress he loved so the great cat took his revenge, now you have invaded his kingdom and killed half of his friends, yet you still claim vengeance, I'll let you two work it out.'

As George turned around and walked off he heard a scream and again the inevitable squelchy crunch. He did not turn back and look for he did not want to think of his old friend Charles and as they were twins it would have been akin to watching him die again, but he saw clarity in his grief now, it was never George's fault, it was obsession that got them killed and they both should have known better.

If you enjoyed Tiger! Tiger! Tiger! Why not leave a review at your favourite online retailer.

You can find me out more about me and upcoming books at:
www.jon-jon.co.uk

VICTORIAN ADVENTURE STORIES

COMING SOON!

The Jellyset Kid

Meet Warwick, a young boy who after drinking unset Jelly awakes to discover it has set *into* his body giving him superhero like abilities. Struggling to keep his powers a secret whilst trying to win the heart of Faustine, he begins to battle the bad guys but is he the only one out there with superpowers?

Aaron the Alien
Rock of the Gollanollarots

In Rock of the Gollanollarots, Timmy is enlisted to help Aaron find a friend who has gone missing on the planet Nollarot

Upon discovering a barren world has replaced the once vibrant colourful planet, Aaron and Timmy are soon confronted by a terrifying race of unstoppable monsters that have turned the place into a desolate rock wasteland, held captive they must try to escape.

Can Aaron and Timmy escape their captors? What has happened to the planet Nollarot and the Gollanollarots who lived on it? Where is their friend? Can they survive long enough to unravel the mystery?

The terrifying truth is worse than they could ever have imagined ...

Sequels

The Mysterious Murder of Mr Milkzilkerdilk Zooboogadoog!

Prequel

Welcome to Bejjerwejjertejnej

www.aaronthealien.com

Contact Jon-Jon via the following details

Email: JonJonWriting@yahoo.co.uk

www.Jon-Jon.co.uk

www.AarontheAlien.com

www.twitter.com/JonJonWrites

www.Facebook.com/TigerNovel

www.Facebook.com/AarontheAlienBook

Made in the USA
Columbia, SC
21 July 2017